# Plz..

## Kiss me or Kill me

*If you are in love, you need medicine*

# Plz..
# Kiss me or Kill me

*If you are in love, you need medicine*

Mihir Raj

Srishti
PUBLISHERS & DISTRIBUTORS

SRISHTI PUBLISHERS & DISTRIBUTORS
N-16, C. R. Park
New Delhi 110 019
srishtipublishers@gmail.com

First published by Srishti Publishers & Distributors in 2011
Copyright © Mihir Raj, 2011

Typeset in AGaramond 11pt. by Suresh Kumar Sharma at Srishti

This book is dedicated to my Late Sister Mona Di, who is immortal in my heart and my fiancée Mansi, without her tremendous support and care, this book could never be imagined. She is also the first reader of my drafts and a wonderful person who always kept standing by my side in my bad days.

# Prologue

It was probably the worst day of my life. Shivani was lying in ICU in a coma and now Rahul too had got admitted to the hospital. He was among those badly injured in the Sarojini Nagar bomb blast which had completely shaken Delhi.

We, the final year students of medicine, were given duty in our hospital to not only attend to the casualties but also learn how to deal with medical emergencies. I was already half out of my mind due to Shivani as she was on life support. How could Robin and I bear to see our sister in such a grim condition? Our eyes were red shot and dry. Dry because we hadn't had proper sleep for consecutive nights and secondly because our lacrimal glands which secretes tear had temporarily stopped functioning.

I was totally startled to see Rahul's parents in such a pathetic condition standing at the hospital gate. Robin and I had rushed to them fearing the worst.

"Aunty, what happened?"

"Raj.. Somebody called us on your uncle's mobile and informed that Rahul has been severely injured in the Sarojini Nagar bomb blast and is being brought here."

"Whaat? Rahul… he did not tell us that he was going Sarojini Nagar," Robin said. "Aunty we had lunch together today and when he was leaving he didn't say he was going to Sarojini Nagar," I said

"It is your good luck that he didn't tell you, at least you people are safe, my sons…" aunty said between sobs.

Soon many ambulances started to arrive. The injured persons were being taken to the hospital wards. Seeing Rahul's unconscious body being placed on a stretcher we just lost our senses. His parents ran towards the stretcher but we stood rooted to the spot unable to believe that it was Rahul with whom we had lunch just four hours back, being carried on a stretcher. Shivani's Rahul ....who too was struggling between life and death since the last two days. Suddenly we started running alongside his stretcher and rushed him to the emergency ward.

Medical profession is not an easy one as you come across suffering and pain everyday till it becomes part of your life. But now we were not just medicos but a friend and a brother. Robin and I were being governed by the same feeling. After a few hours when the doctor said Rahul was responding to treatment Robin soothed Rahul's parents to calm down. We requested them to go back home and take rest as we were there to take care of Rahul. But aunty refused to leave Rahul's side. Somehow Robin arranged a sofa for her in Rahul's ward. Utterly exhausted Robin and I sat down in a sofa in the main hall. Really , the whole thing was something which I had never imagined in my wildest dream.... that two love birds would one day be struggling for life at the same time in the same hospital with some same common faces!!

Love is a wonderful feeling as it gives you many beautiful moments worth living but the path through which it moves is not easy. Many past memories started flashing in my mind and started tormenting me. I suddenly went down memory where I saw myself, Robin, Rahul, Shivani, Charulata, Ankita Madam and our days in medical college "DIMS". My memory started craving all those beautiful moments of Love and its magic but sometimes its result is really not within our reach. We love without bothering about the misery later. Lastly I concluded, **"If you are in love, you need medicine"**

# *Acknowledgement*

This is a fiction and my book but it will be a little injustice if I call it just my book and not my dream. This dream came true when I was supported by some divine forces and people around me so generous and wonderful. It's my pleasure to thank:

- Almighty, the divine God, who always blessed me with positive energy and inspiration and a power of self motivation.

- My parents; My father Sri Saket Bihari Shukla and my Mom Smt. Aasha Shukla who not only supported me in every sense and nurtured me but tolerated me, as tolerating such an erratic son is sometimes impossible.

- I would like to thank my darling younger brother 'Sameer', who is just Lakshman to me; however I could never be Ram.

- My Grandparents Sri R.S Thakur and Smt Lalita Thakur. I am blessed enough to have such a grandparents.

- My Grandparents Sri Shivratna Shukla and Smt Rajkumari Shukla for those wonderful stories that they narrated me in my childhood which somewhere made me a writer.

- My maternal uncle Sri S Kumar, who is one of the great persons, who inspired me a lot.

- Darpi, my domestic helper, but more than a relative to me and my Guru Dhruvdev Lal; both of them are now no more but still alive in my heart.

- My editor Mrs. Gitanjali Chatterjee, who worked really hard and made this book readable.

- Entire team of Srishti Publishers, who supported me from the very first meeting. It is really what I call a destiny.

- My teachers, relatives and friends who showed their great faith on me.

- Mohit Bhaia, my ex roommate who provided me such a calm environment in room to pen down my imaginations in sentences.

- My laptop for working nonstop whenever I was driven crazy by black coffee to write this book.

- Last but not the least I would like to thank you for holding this book in your hands without your support and love I can't achieve the status of a well known writer.

# Beginning: A Reality

DIMS... Delhi Institute of Medical Science. A dream place for many medical aspirants. It's a bitter truth that80 per cent of Indian students want to be a doctor or engineer as if there is no other option. In fact it's not their fault. Most parents and relatives judge a kid's intelligence on the basis of what he wants to become in future. If the child says a doctor or an engineer, he is labeled as very intelligent. Children are in fact forced to give such answers lest they are thought less intelligent than the child next door. If at age of seven or eight children are victims of inferiority complex, you can imagine how bright their future will be?

When I was very young my father who was also my first ever teacher, told me, "Dear son, there is only two things which you can be in future ——either a doctor or an IAS..."

I saw a great expectation in my father's eye for me. My father was unlike other fathers. He at least gave me two choices and also time to time tried his level best to make me understand what a doctor and

IAS is? By sheer virtue of his attempts I was convinced and doctors in white apron with a stethoscope around their neck started appealing to me greatly.

I tried hard but couldn't make it to the merit list even after two attempts. It was hard for my family to get a seat for me through management quota or by paying donation. A series of meetings started in the family and after a few of these meetings it was decided that I would have to be sent to a medical college. Father talked to the management and they offered me a seat on a self-financing scheme. The session was to begin on 1ˢᵗ September. That was how I came to this wonderful dreamland called DIMS...

From my observation I identified three groups in the college. The first group consisted of the intelligent boys and girls. They used to be the cream whose names used to decorate the college's merit list. In other words they had come through tough brain storming pre medical test.

The second group consisted of mischievous and dull students. They were kids of political bigwigs or business tycoons. They had come just for the heck of it and to make the college management wealthier. They used to be drunk most of the times and sometimes came like that even to class. They had no problems about taking drugs.

However it was the third group which was the most interesting. It was a group of semi studious and semi virtuous young men. This group was interesting because not were they just good in studies but excelled in other activities as well. In other words, you can say they were Bindas Bandes who were not only interested in stressing their brain on huge books of anatomy etc. but also they wanted to live life to the full. The third group fascinated me.

It was my first day in medical college, I was very excited and in my excitement I reached the lecture hall before anyone. I couldn't believe that I was to attend my first medical lecture today. I made up my mind to be a good student and not repeat any of the mistakes I had made earlier.

There was a great struggle to get hostel seat. As I had not been allotted a hostel room yet I was staying in Munirka as a paying guest in Rahul's house. Rahul was my class mate and a great mystery; even after a great deal of effort I couldn't fathom his area of interest. Till now he was very gentle and polite and spoke little. His mother was a very generous lady and was a mother figure to me. After two months I got a room in the hostel, but by then I had developed a strong bond with Rahul's family and I used to visit them when ever I got time.

Man is a social animal I had read somewhere and I realized how true it was. In the first year generally students get into relationships with fellow students, but it is also true, that the waves of time wash away many of these relationships and compel us to make some new ones depending upon our needs.

# Medical college: An introduction

Medical college is really an amazing place. You can see small groups   every where enjoying in their own way, but to tell you frankly girls to them were the most exciting. Except for a few guys, every other guy was interested in girls. Those few guys needless to mention were gay.  For them girls didn't exist.

I was getting very worried about getting a seat in the hostel. One day finally I asked the management whether I would get a room in the hostel or not?

"Today we are going to put up a new list on the notice board, check if your roll number is there or not."

At 9 am sharp lecture started.  Dr.Harikant Shastri MBBS, MS, PHD. As I entered the lecture room it was the first thing I noticed on the green board. I felt that he was not a professor but Yamraaj himself coming to deliver a lecture. The lecture hall was very noisy; students were speculating something or the other about Dr. Shastri.

"I have heard he is a very tough teacher, a khadhoos type man."

"Getting even pass mark is very difficult in his subject I believe," added another.

One thing very interesting I heard among the many things spoken about him was, "While praying he does not read the Chalisa but the damn Anat book."

These words were enough to fill us with a sense of foreboding and curiosity about him. Suddenly the lecture hall became silent. Yamraaj…. I mean Dr. Shastri …. Entered

"I will not waste time in introducing myself as you people have already wasted enough time gathering information about me. I tell you very frankly, nothing will help you here except hard work so let's begin with some introduction to Anatomy."

Every one became serious.

"Anatomy…. Let's start with its definition. Who will tell me its definition?"

Only a few hands rose up. I knew the definition but I didn't dare to raise my hand.

Finally, a guy started defining Anatomy.

"It is the science which deals with the study of….."

"Stop, stop……. Let's play a game."

"You all will write a few interesting words for me. Don't worry; I just want to know how strong your English is?"

"Write the words stethoscope, surgeon, hypognathous…"

"Write your name and roll number on your paper and submit it to me after writing these words."

A few students wrote as fast as they could and submitted it to Prof Shastri, as if one who was to give it first would receive an award.

Dr. Shastri looked down to check the papers. After ten minutes he looked up and said, "It was expected that this year too we will have many idiots who can't even write a single medical terminology correctly."

"It's a matter of great sorrow that most of you even don't know how to write the word surgeon….. And you idiots are hoping to be surgeons one day…. not only surgeons but great surgeons. I see only five papers here which are correct. It shows how the standard is going down day by day and we are producing muggers only, " he said in disgust.

"Now I am going to read out those five names. They may please stand up."

"Manas, Suneet, Manzar, Rahul, Rajvardhan Sahay"

The last mentioned name was mine.

All five of us stood up.

"I congratulate you people as you all have unnecessary edge on all other idiots."

Till today I have been unable to make out whether Dr. Shastri actually congratulated us or pulled our leg.

"Anatomy is not just a science, it is a vast deep ocean, the more you will dive in it more you will get closer to it, but sorry to say even a whole life isn't enough for mastering Anatomy. One can't become a good surgeon without having good knowledge of anatomy. A surgeon without an excellent knowledge of Anatomy is like a flower without fragrance. The choice is yours what you want to be — A natural rose or an artificial one."

The class ended with some introduction about anatomy as a science. Those four hours were really grueling and after getting out of the lecture hall we were surprised to find that we were still alive after the brain –sapping lecture of Shastri. We just trooped out to do some window shopping.

Next day I saw my roll number in the hostel list. I was very happy. I rushed to  the administrative block After showing  them my particulars they handed me a receipt and  the details about my room.

"Kabir hostel… room number 19. It's a 2 seater"

"What? A 2 seater? Sir, but I had applied for a single seater," I said angrily.

"So what, young man…. For your information we don't provide single seaters till the 2ⁿᵈ year, and so consider yourself lucky….. Many are still in the wait list."

I understood the situation and taking the keys from him hastily moved towards my hostel.

"Room no 19… here it is."

One name was written at the door in bold letters —Robin Raman **Singh**. The Singh was in bold   as if this Singh was the king of the hostel.

 We were being given   a practical demonstration of anatomy. I had got somewhat late for class. As I entered the class room I was surprised to see a few teary eyed students. I guessed something was amiss. It was Dr. Shastri's class.

"What happened?"I whispered to Manas.

"Welcome Rajvardhan Saheb… I love late comers." Shastri sir said with a terrific sarcasm.

"Sir actually I…" I tried to explain but Dr Shastri interrupted me and said, "I hate explanations, you are late means you are late, doesn't matter why you are late."

After a few minutes even my eyes started smarting. It was formalin. I kept rubbing my eyes.

"Put your bloody hands down and concentrate only on what I am saying," Dr. Shastri roared.

Putting my hand down and with tearful eyes I tried to concentrate on what Dr. Shastri was explaining.

Ragging was at its peak in the college. Someone narrated how a few seniors had entered their hostel last night and ragged him. They had given him a match stick and asked him to measure the length and width of the corridor. They even snipped off some of his hair. Not only me but my mother too was worried about me being ragged.

It was lunch break. After having lunch I went to the library to issue a book. The library was on the fifth floor. I heard some strange noises outside. After finding the book I peeped out of the window. I saw a gathering of at least a hundred students and they were shouting as if there was a boxing match going on. I was afraid of gatherings as it used to be the synonym of ragging. We had Biochem lecture just now, and the place of gathering was near the lecture hall, so unwillingly I had to go towards lecture hall. With each step my heart beats became faster. The intensity of the noise was also increasing. I couldn't stop myself and I entered the crowd. I saw a guy standing in front of a chair on which a thick slab of glass was placed and to my utter surprise he was going to break it with his hands in karate style. I saw some seniors surrounding that guy and in between they were shouting "Rajpoot…he… he… Rajpoot". I didn't understand anything so I tried to understand. The guy hammered his hand on the slab but it didn't break but his hand started to bleed. In a fraction of second before we realized slab didn't break, he hammered one more time and the slab broke into three pieces but his hand was badly injured.

"Rajpoot sirf kehne ka hi nai sach me hoon," he shouted.

Suddenly all became quiet. I don't know what happened to me, I took out my hanky and ran towards him. I bandaged his hand but he was not looking at me. He was staring at the seniors. Prof C.K Chawla at once arrived there and within a minute the place became empty.

"What happened to you?" he asked that guy.

"Nothing Sir…Actually I had a purulent wound and by mistake I crushed it so pus with blood is oozing out of it," he replied smartly.

"Are you sure it is a wound or any bloody ragger was here?" he asked

"No sir, nothing like that."

"You….. Help him to the medical room," he pointed towards me. I left him in the medical room and returned to attend the lecture. We got a fifteen minute break and I asked Manas, "What was going on there?"

"Why that guy exhibited such foolishness?"

"I also don't know that guy but I think some seniors had any back account with the guy, they were ragging him," Manas said.

"To harm someone is not ragging yaar," I said.

"Actually seniors had asked him to snatch a senior girl's dupatta," Manas said.

"What? What are these rascals asking to do? This is negative ragging," I said in anger.

"Ragging can't be positive bro…. this guy refused to do that and said Rajpoots never disgrace a girl, they fight for their prestige."

"Seniors said ok if you are Rajpoot show us you are really one and asked him to break the slab of glass in one shot by hand"

"Oh… but he did it in the second attempt, seniors will have a point again," I said.

"Ya, even I think so… but bro you must take care as you helped that guy so now you too will be in their hit list," Manas alarmed me. I lost myself in some unknown fear. After class I first went to Munirka, collected my luggage and shifted to the hostel. I knocked the room which was half open. A guy came to me with half closed eyes.

"Hi… I am Rajvardhan Sahay… this room has been allotted to me by administration," I said.

As we saw each other we said in unison "You?"

"My name is Robin Raman Singh"

"So you are Robin?" I asked with mixed feeling.

"Yes smarty…."

"Unwillingly I forwarded my hand for hand shake."

He first forwarded his hand but it was totally injured. I pulled my hands back.

"Koi baat nahi smarty, gale lag ja," he said and hugged me.

Robin helped me in arranging my stuff. It was hard to believe on two things which were going in my mind at the same time. First, I will have to share the room with some one and second, which I guess was more problematic, that I was going to stay with a foolish Rajpoot, whose ego comes first above everything. For me such people were psychos and staying with a psycho was impossible. I lay down on the bed and started thinking, how to change my room.

# Ragging: Jab I saw her

I spent a few days with him unwillingly but soon Robin's personality started impressing me. He never believed in unnecessary showing off— something which used to be there in every second student of this college, although he was a son of politician. His father was a Member of Parliament from Jamui, a district in Bihar.

One night few of our seniors came to Kabir hostel which was allotted to us 1st year students. Soon there was a panic in Kabir hostel as at least fifty students including me became the victim of ragging. Robin was lucky as he was out that night. He was at his local guardian's residence in Mukherjee Nagar. That day I knew what ragging is all about. It is obeying your seniors without applying your brain. We were asked to take off our cloths. Now the hall of Kabir house was full of fifty grown up guys completely naked. I had never imagined myself in such a humiliating condition even in my wildest dream.

One of them called a guy among us and said, "Muthh marta hai?"

"Muthh???" He muttered the word in a confusing tone.

"Ya muthh... Hand practice..Masturbate..." he explained.

"Yes... sometimes," he stammered.

"Do it for us right now, chanting "apna haath jagarnath," he commanded.

He encircled his glans and acted like that saying the above dialogue.

Ragging was not over as yet. We were asked to stand in a line facing another's back and bums. That day I felt that the parts of the body we keep covered is very sensitive and it should be exposed to only our respective partner for whom it is meant.

One of the senior asked us to bow down and hold each others scrotum and take four rounds of the hall raising the slogan "long live our seniors". If you will imagine this posture you must crack into laughter but in reality we were dying several deaths with each passing second. Those nude twenty minutes will remain a nightmare in my life. In between a few seniors used to stroke the asses of those they thought worth touching. Fortunately my ass didn't attract any of them.

Robin was a normal guy until you did not put his Rajput ego in between him and the world outside. Then he becomes impossible. A few students of our course used to take undue advantage of it. The whole 1st year was unhappy with the seniors about ragging and they were also jealous that Robin had escaped. They thought to do something against the leader of the seniors who had humiliated us by ordering us to take off our clothes and parade around the hall naked the scrotum holding incident. For taking revenge they chose Robin as he was the only who didn't face that ragging and most important that he was the only guy who had the guts to do something against them and also he could be easily incited just by challenging his Rajput ego. They told him about the humiliating episode and incited him against them.

"You were also the victim of that opprobrious ragging… why didn't you tell me?" he asked me in anger.

"I didn't tell you as it was not a pleasant experience and secondly I know you, uselessly you will do something what I don't want." I replied

"Certainly I will , I am  not  going to spare them," he said angrily.

I tried a lot to convince him but he was not ready to listen.

A few days were left for the fresher's party and then no ragging. I used to be very cautious but one day I was caught by those seniors who had asked Robin to break the glass slab. Manas was right when he had said that they will rag me later for helping Robin.

"You Junior… come here," one of them shouted at me.

"Me?" I asked

"Ya you... Come here."

"That day you helped that guy but now who will help you?" one said.

I kept standing keeping my mouth shut as I knew a word from me could push me in a more severe situation.

"You look handsome like a chocolaty hero of bollywood. We just give you a routine bollywood scene of proposing to a girl with a red rose, show us your talent."

One of them pushed a red rose in my hand and pointed his finger towards a girl whom I was to propose. I could not see the girl as she was standing very far, her back towards us.

"We will see you from here only how well you act?" one of them said.

"Go now and show us your talent."

I was really nervous as I had never proposed to a girl before and I was sure I would be kicked by that girl. Same time I was thanking God that they did not asked me to do some uncivilized act like snatching the girl's dupatta or some such thing.

With each step towards the girl my blood pressure rose and I was close to fainting. I made up my mind what I would say and how I would present myself to the girl. Finally I reached near her.

"Excuse me ma'am…." I stuttered in embarrassment and fear.

The girl turned and said, "Yes?"

When I saw the girl's face it seemed I was not on earth but some where else in a fairy land. My God….how beautiful she was?

Can a girl be so beautiful that her mesmerizing beauty will transport me to another world? I was staring at her without blinking my eyelids.

"Hello… May I help you?"

At once I regained my composure and said, "Yes ma'am, only you can help me."

"Tell me how?"She asked.

"As you know ragging is at its peak and I am one of the victims of today's ragging. The people sitting there asked me to propose you with this rose," I explained.

"Ok, I get you… no problem. Give me this flower and tell them I refused your proposal," she said with a naughty smile.

Though she was helping me, for a second I felt bad when she said 'tell them I refused your proposal'.

"Thank you very much ma'am," I said and handed over the rose to her.

Thus I got rid of this fragile ragging in which I was sure to be slapped but by destiny I met the girl who made my heartbeats faster. I just kept thinking about her first look.

In the evenings I used to play cricket after college everyday. It was just near to our library and a good practice ground. I was hitting well but got bowled out when I glimpsed a girl at the library floor. She was the same girl whom I had proposed earlier in the day today. I became restless, I wanted to talk to her but I did not have any valid reason. I wished any of the seniors would once again ask me to propose to her. My helplessness didn't allow me to approach her.

# Jab I saw her Again

We were having our first trimester exam so I used to be in the library for studying. We were preparing for our first trimester exams.

"So today you are here?"

I raised my head to see who it was.

"Ma'am... you here...?" I stammered.

"Why? You are surprised? I come here everyday but I am seeing you here first time t" she said with a smile.

"Ya... I usually play cricket at this time"

"May I seat here?" she asked.

"Ya, sure... sure ma'am"

I was very conscious of her while replying to her. That day we had only formal greetings as she was very serious and began reading but I became totally restless as I could smell her hair and from that short distance and totally lost my concentration.

It was a troublesome evening before the exam day. Everybody was sitting with their books open, but Robin was resting with a smiling face.

"Robin? Are you alright?" I asked.

He was thinking something deeply I guessed as he did not respond.

"Robin?" I shouted.

"Ya… ya... What happened Raj?" he responded.

"I am asking you that. What happened?"

"Raj, I must confess to you that I am in love." he said.

"Are you crazy? We have exam tomorrow and here you are thinking of love?" I said.

"Yaar... I think I am in love with her?"

"With whom?" I asked being irritated.

"Charulata… ya, that's her name."

"But she is our senior," he added.

"How you concluded you are in love with her? Does she know about it?" I asked him.

"No yaar but you remember once seniors asked me to snatch a girl's dupatta? It was Charulata's. Best thing is that when she knew I refused to do that and instead of that I preferred to break the slab, she asked many girls of our class about me" he said in excitement.

"So what are your plans?" I asked

"Nothing much right now I am taking all pleasures of this newly discovered love," he said running a combing through his hair.

"Concentrate on your exam Robin as Shastri is going to kill us afterwards."

"Exams are just part of studies, so I am not worried about it. What

I am really worried about is my lovely heart which is no more mine," he mumbled.

Our trimester exams and practical works were now over. Two things disturbed us a lot. First the exams and second these seniors. We were ragged at least twice a day and in between we had to prepare for exams. I cracked up several times in the toilet. Most unfortunate thing was that even toilets used to be fully packed as it was perhaps the safest place in any hostel where our seniors could not disturb us. We used to sit there several hours preparing for the exams and to save ourselves from cruel ragging. After exams there was leave for five days and first year students dispersed somewhere to get rid of ragging. On the 6th day we had the Fresher's party and after that no ragging. Robin too went to his sister's house in Rohini.

I had only one abode and that was Rahul's home. I went there and aunty led me to the room in which I used to stay. After me they just aborted the idea of keeping a PG. It was really nice to be at home after such a tiring and restless schedule of exams and ragging.

At night I had dinner with Rahul's family.

"Raj, after your going it seems as we have only one son," aunty lamented while serving food.

"Why do you think like this aunty .Doesn't matter where I am…I will be your second son in every condition."

"That's true beta but you know your aunty, how emotional she is?" uncle added.

"I never feel Rahul's presence in the house although he is at home most of the time after college"

I looked at Rahul with complaining eyes but perhaps he had no care for all these conversations as he was pretty busy finishing his dinner.

"He made his presence felt last time when he was twelve years old," aunty said

Morning used to be very calm and refreshing and local guys used to play cricket in a field not very far so I planned to join them as this game was my weakness. Suddenly our game was interrupted by a sky blue color Maruti Zen as it entered the boundary line.

"Please move out of the boundary," I shouted.

"Sorry... Give us just 5 minutes," a girl's voice came from the opposite side.

I was just discussing the game with my team and suddenly someone asked, "Please help us."

As I turned it became the first pleasant surprise of that morning. She was the same senior girl.

"Oh my God…… You?" I exclaimed.

"You!!!!! I can't believe it" she too exclaimed.

"But by the way why you said OH MY GOD……" she asked.

I went to sleep thinking of her and in the morning here she was in front of me. Was it not less than any miracle but how I could tell her this? So I tried to pretend.

"Actually I never imagined that I can see you ever in a cricket ground as you are a book worm," I said

"By the way what you are doing here, ma'am?"

"My car is not getting started and the mechanics shop is a little far, can you guys help me push my car to the shop?"

"Come on guys, we have an assignment this morning. Just push the car till the repair shop."

Our game was over for that day and perhaps for the first time I was happy being interrupted. We were all set to push the car and she was still by my side.

"Go and control the steering as the car can not control it," I said.

"Don't worry, my friend is there for controlling the steering but if you don't want me to stand by your side and want to put some more weight in the car then I am going and sitting inside," she said and turned towards the car.

I don't know why but in a reflex action I just grabbed her hand and stopped her.

She looked at me totally surprised.

"I am sorry ma'am… I thought you are alone and I have no problem if you stand by my side but why are you bothering yourself as its far, you may sit inside," I said

"Are you sure? I think you are not. By the way you gripped my hand very tightly it seems you have never held a girl's hand ever," she said and laughed.

I was pushing the car and in between looking at her and several times I found she too looking at me and when our eyes met I used to look down and she used to smile.

Why were you surprised to see me at the ground?" I asked

"It was just because of the fact that I had never imagined a guy may be that crazy about cricket" she said and smiled.

I didn't say anything. We had reached the mechanics shop. I was a bit disappointed as it was the time to say bye to her.

"So…"

"So what?" she replied at once.

"I think I should leave now as your car is at the repairing center," I stammered.

"No way… We will have tea first and then if you want you may leave," she said.

"Why you are troubling yourself. There is no need for it," I said reluctantly.

Meanwhile  the other guys shouted "But we want tea."

"See your friends also want to have tea, by the way for your information I must tell you one can not have a better tea anywhere in south Delhi than here," she said.

There was a small dhaba there. All the guys entered except me and her. She too turned towards the dhaba but I was still motionless. She came back and grabbed my hand and pulled me to the dhaba.

We were having our tea. She was right. It was the best tea I had ever had. Perhaps all credit goes to the company and the girl sitting so close to me that at the mere turning of our body our shoulders kissed each other.

"So you are enjoying your mini vacation?" she asked me.

"Ya… It's really good to enjoy outdoors our vacation after exams"

"Are you planning to go out of station?" she asked.

"No… I am staying at Rahul's home as hostel condition is not good for freshers"

"Ya, you are right. It's the high time of ragging in our hostel too. Girls are being mercilessly ragged by seniors," she informed.

I always used to think there was no ragging in girls' hostel.

"How these guys enter in your hostel?" I asked in astonishment.

"Girls rag girls dear…. Not guys," she said.

I had the feeling like even gals don't have heart.

"But guys can also enter our girl's hostel, it's not a problem at all," she said mischievously.

"How? There is a tight security at the gate" I said

"Ya but not at the back gate... There are many ways to come in. Some prefer climbing water pipes," she laughed and said.

"So you come here daily to play cricket" she asked.

"No, today was the first day but I guess I will be here daily till vacation," I informed her.

"What were you doing here?" I asked.

"I was just learning driving from my friend," she said and introduced me to her friend.

The day passed just in her sweet memories. There was a driving force inside me which was letting my soul fly out of my body and dance with her soul somewhere in wonderland. We met almost every morning but not for more than five minutes. I tell you honestly those five minutes used to be the most beautiful time of my day for which I used to wait all 23 hours and 55 minutes. Our mini vacation ended and it was again the same boring and tough life of medicine but before that the "Fresher's party".

# A Perfect Romantic night

We were desperately waiting for the evening to come as it meant end of our ragging. That evening was great. It was the first week of November. Evening was very fine as if romance had every reason to cherish itself. I was just restless to go to the party not because the party was going to rock the floor but to have a glimpse of the girl for whom my heart beat furiously. Unfortunately till that time I didn't know her name even. Our seniors had booked a disco at PVR Priyas for the evening Robin and I reached there at time as Robin was a very punctual guy. Sometimes it used to suck me. By 7:30 everyone including our hosts and guests were at the floor but my eyes were still searching for her elegant presence. We were just greeting each other and the seniors apologized for all worst moments of ragging and also wishing us all the best in medical school. It was really nice to have those seniors wish us who were just shrinking from them till this evening.

All it happens in medical school which if finishes with a good end makes life live with Great Spirit and if bad ending then a hell. As I was still to conclude the end of our ragging a soft voice which was very much familiar to me vibrated in my ears.

Here comes the lady. Perhaps I don't have all the magical words to describe her but she was looking absolutely ravishing. In a short pink party gown, a few strands moist hair kissing her cheeks which were like the moon is covered partially from both ends with black clouds. Her smooth lips glistened with a pink glister which was enough to kill me. Not just me but everyone around was just mesmerized with her beauty. Soon she was surrounded by her friends and I was dying to catch another glimpse of her. Robin too was looking that side. The party began and every body started enjoying.

"Let's have some whisky" Robin said touching my shoulders.

"Ya… sure. You wait I will bring it for you" I said and moved toward the counter.

I offered the glass of whisky to Robin.

"Won't you have it?" he asked

"Yaar I am not in a mood today" I replied. "I am already intoxicated."

"How? You had it before the party?"

"No man… I am just not in my senses… I have been robbed by someone's beauty," I said

"Oh great…propose to her today as you will not get a better chance than this," he suggested.

"How can I? Till today I don't even know her name in spite of a few brief meetings," I said in irritation.

"Very slow, my friend…If you will do like that only some other guy will come and snatch her away," he said and finished his glass.

"Get me another?" he said

I brought one more peg for him.

"Raj... I too have thought to propose her today," he said

"You will propose to her in this condition?" I said with surprise.

"Yes, what's wrong? Girls don't mind as they don't have a mind and secondly today my courage is not supporting me to propose to her. Only this wine can help me, in other words fati padi hai yaar…" he said and tried to move forward but staggered. I held him.

"No need… I am fine... I wish she would hold me now," he said.

After two pegs Robin became impossible. Few guys came and started talking to Robin and I moved towards the wine counter thinking whether wine could help me too as I too was short of courage. Most of the people were at the dance floor. Some couples were intimately sitting with each other in some corner.

"Russian vodka," I ordered.

"One for me too," someone ordered.

"Ma'am …you...?" I was surprised.

"Ya... me... why are you surprised? Cant I have a drink?" she asked

"Ya... ya ... of course. Only thing I thought you don't drink."

"Why you thought so? This is the problem, why people take me like that"

"Do you also feel I am a behnjee type girl?" she asked

"No… but ya, I took you to be traditional Indian girl who doesn't drink."

"How do I look today?" she asked swirling her body to the left and right

"An absolutely Indian beauty …in other words —stunning…"

She poured the entire contents of the glass in her mouth and immediately coughed and spluttered as it did not seem to agree to the mucous membrane in her mouth. I too swallowed my drink in one shot as my prestige was at stake.

"I feel like vomiting" she complained.

"What?" I couldn't say more than that.

"Where is the wash room?" she asked keeping her hands on her mouth.

"Come with me," I held one of her arms and guided her to the wash room.

She went inside and poured out every thing she had taken that day.

We were again near the bar.

"I am going to have one more peg . You too want to have another," I asked sarcastically

"No...No... I am dying."

"So... will you dance or will keep standing here all night?" she asked.

"I can't dance," I replied.

"Huh… I know you are my junior but we can dance and you must dance," she said and started pulling me towards the dance floor.

She started moving imposingly. Now perhaps vodka started showing its effect and I too started dancing but an arm's distance was always there between us. In between I used to look around for people's reaction. I saw Robin looking at me once or twice.

"Its suffocating here... let's go out." she said.

"But where?" I asked.

"Anywhere… but not here. It's too noisy."

I got something which I had never expected. A walk in the night with a lady, whom just by seeing my body and soul rocked internally. I asked Rahul for his bike and he at once handed me the keys.

We came out of party hall and I moved towards the bike. It was a moonlit night which seemed to have become more special because of the girl beside me. I moved towards parking.

"Where are you going?" She asked.

"Bike is there..." I replied.

"I will not sit on your bike," she said.

"Why? Anyway, it's not my bike" I said with disappointment.

"I don't sit on anybody else's bike except my brother's and father's," she clarified.

"But why you want to ride a bike? Isn't it a very special night and the wind is also cold?" she said

For the first time noticed the wind was fast and really cold. I came to her and waited for her upcoming desire or in other words order.

"Let's move around... I never enjoyed night life" she said and moved towards Barista.

I followed her. I was walking a little behind her.

"Are you with me or are you alone?" she asked turning back.

"I am pretty much with you" I said and ran to fill in the distance.

"Tell me something about yourself?" she asked with a smile.

"What do you want to know?"

"Anything interesting about you but first about your family?" she said.

"Well... You know my name; I am a native of Bihar. In my family including me and my parents I have a younger brother. He is in the 12th standard" I said.

"What else you want to know?" I asked.

"It's enough about your family. Now tell me about yourself," she said.

"I don't know about myself much so I may tell you something wrong," I replied. "But you can ask what you want to know."

"Ok... What you do except play cricket?" she asked sarcastically.

"Except that it's really difficult to say. Like all medicos I go to college and nothing special as such," I replied.

"Don't you have any girl friend?" she asked looking straight at me.

For the first time, I became afraid of her big beautiful eyes and stammered, "No..... Till today I am single."

"Single? Why?" she asked.

"Do you have a boy friend?" I asked with unknown fear.

"Right now you will answer my questions, you can't ask questions now" she stared me.

"You never tried for any girl?" she asked.

We decided to move towards JNU campus.

"No... I am afraid of refusal," I replied.

"Did you like someone ever?" she asked.

"As such I liked many girls but it was only an infatuation," I replied.

"What is love according to you?" she asked.

"Love is... a ... aa... something aa... a..." I stammered.

I thought I was suffering from aphasia.

"Ok, no problem... you can define it later," she said and smiled.

I was relieved.

We were at Ganga dhaba. It was 12 o' clock and the dhaba was still crowded.

"I want to eat something," she said.

"Ok... I will bring it for you. What do you want to have?" I asked.

"Paratha sabji with tea," she replied.

I managed to get a plate of paratha and sabji and two cups of tea. All the rocks where people use to sit near the dhaba were occupied with couples and other groups. We couldn't find any rock to sit on so we moved towards Ganga hostel. Near the gate of the hostel there is a slab where people can sit. The cold wind was now fiercer and her hair which was dry now was blowing arbitrarily. She placed the plate on the rock and started eating. She was looking so beautiful and innocent while eating and in between managing her hair entering her mouth as the wind was kissing them. Really I was jealous of the wind which in front of me was daring to kiss my girl. For a few moments she forgot I was with her. Once she looked up and said "Oh I am sorry... won't you eat?"

"No, I am not hungry .I am enjoying my tea" I replied.

She again started concentrating on her parathas and I totally on her.

Suddenly the moon hid behind the clouds and started playing hide and seek with the clouds but who cares for that moon when a living moon was in front of me and I was enjoying each and every gesture of hers.

Suddenly she said, "Can you tie up my hair?"

"What? Me? I don't know how to do it," I said

It was really difficult to make out if it was real or I was dreaming

… and that too so sweet. I wanted to touch her hair and I cursed myself for refusing.

"You can do it… its not difficult. These idiots are coming in my mouth," she said.

"In my purse you will find a hair band" she said pointing towards her bag.

Somehow I managed to find the hair band.

"Why are you standing? Tie it," she ordered.

I moved towards her beautiful silky hair with trembling hands as if I was suffering from cerebellum tremor. Several times I tried to gather all the hair but in between many used to slip from my grip. She was perhaps enjoying my pathetic condition.

At last when I had managed to gather all tightly and she cried "Ouch!" and I left it all.

"What will you do? You can't even handle a girl's hair, how you will handle a girl someday as they are more complicated then their hair," she said smiling and looked at me.

"Give it another try," she suggested.

This time I somehow managed to tie them all up but not completely. After few minutes she was all done with her dinner. She washed her hands and tried to find her hanky in her bag.

"Where has it gone? It's really a mess inside," she murmured.

I found not only hair and but everything associated with girls are complicated. Finally she looked at me and I offered my hanky to her which she took hesitantly. Suddenly she screamed and started jumping, her body brushed several times with mine.

"What happened?" I threw my tea and asked.

She did not say anything but keep jumping up and down holding up her dress. She stretched it and looked inside in. I saw her pink bra and at once turned away my face.

"What happened?" I asked again.

"Shut up... Don't you see something has gone inside, I can feel it," she said.

She saw me turning in the other direction and said "Oh... I am sorry..."

She brought a dead ant from inside and showed it to me innocently. "This was inside, but its dead now."

"No problem, it is quite obvious as he tried to explore the wrong place," I said.

We both laughed and then we sat there for another hour and during which time I told her at least ten definitions of love. These were partially or completely rejected by her. It was now 2 o' clock. She looked at her watch and screamed once again, "Oh my God its 2 ... my friends will be worrying about me"

"Send them an SMS saying you are alright," I suggested.

"No... Let's move to the party venue," she said.

As we exited the JNU gate a few big drops of rain fell on us.

"Oh no...Is it raining?" she asked.

"Perhaps," I said.

"But its November," she said being irritated.

"Ya... It's not usual but it's called the October heat," I replied.

"No... November heat," she said again in irritation and hastened her steps. All the way she was quiet and I tried to catch up with her. I was feeling bad as my beautiful time was coming to its end with each step of hers. I felt helpless. A few more drops fell and it turned her face red hot. When we were a little away from Vasant Continental it started raining torrentially. She looked at me and I held her hands and made her run inside Vasant Continental. The guard stopped us. I convinced the guard to let us stand there until the rain stopped. I came near her and saw her shivering in cold as she was totally wet. She was caressing her body with her hands. She was looking more beautiful than a red rose drenched in winter dews. Her guan was totally sticking to her skin and her figure was no more unknown to me. In between she tried to adjust her gown.

"Here, I will go and fetch my coat from the bike, you are shivering" I said and moved away from her.

She held my hand and said "Don't leave me alone, I am scared."

"Its not very far. Don't worry I will be back soon," I said and tried to free myself from her grip.

I collected my coat from the dickey of the bike and rushed towards Vasant Continental. When I put the coat around her she looked at me with completely different eyes.

"Don't you feel cold, you too are totally wet?" she asked buttoning up the coat.

"No I am alright... I am not a delicate doll," I said considering myself like a bollywood hero.

"Are you trying to impress me?" she giggled.

I didn't reply.

That stupid rain didn't continue more than twenty minutes.

"I want to go back to the hostel as I have a headache. I think I am going to get fever. Can you drop me at my hostel?" she asked.

"Yes, sure. I too want to go back to hostel," I was totally delighted.

We moved towards the bike and then I said, "I hope you wouldn't mind sitting on my bike?"

She sat like all girls with both legs on one side but for that she had to hold my shoulders and she did. I was totally intoxicated with her touch. All the way she didn't say a word. I dropped her at Indira hostel.

"So...?" she said

"So..?." I couldn't say anything.

"How do you rate your time today?" she asked.

"It was like a dream. How about you?" I asked hopefully.

"I had told you not to ask me any question," she glared at me.

"I am sorry but don't you think its slight injustice as you know so much about me and I still don't know who you are?" I said scratching my head. "I don't even know your name?"

"By the way I want to tell you that all your ten definition were correct but incomplete as love can not be defined in words, it's a different feeling at different situations," she said. "Some day you will definitely know about me, have patience."

"Good night... take care," she said and thrust out her hand for a handshake.

We shook hands. For me it was really two different feelings for two different situations. I was happy to touch her hand and was sad to be leaving. At once my mobile rang. It was Rahul. There was an emergency. Robin and a senior had had a fight. I at once turned my bike towards Priya.

# Night of broken heart & Friendship

$A_s$ I entered the party hall it was as if a storm had just annihilated the surrounding. There was now complete silence. Rahul came to me and narrated what happened.

"Robin had been incited by all the other guys against the senior who ragged you people in the hostel that night. Robin and others gathered masturbated and collected semen in a small bottle and mixed it with the senior's Limca. But another senior had seen it and informed him and a scuffle ensued between Robin and him. We and other seniors managed to separate them but by then both had got hurt."

"Where are those bastards were who incited Robin?" I asked angrily.

They hid themselves that time and left Robin alone to face them.

"Where is Robin?" I asked.

"He is full drunk and sitting at the other end of the hall," Rahul informed.

We quickly moved towards Robin. He saw us and bowed his head down.

"Robin, why did you do it?" I asked.

He didn't reply.

I again asked.

"What's wrong with you?"

At once he stood and slapped me hard.

"Saala, dost bol kar pith pe waar karta hai he muttered viciously.

"What happened? What did I do?" I asked in astonishment.

"Get lost or else I will kill you today," he shouted.

Every body was looking at us. It seemed humiliating but it was not in my hand to escape from such situations. Before I could ask anything he again shouted, "Didn't you know she is Charulata?"

"Who is Charulata?" I asked.

"The girl with whom you flirted all night" he said and stepped forward as if to slap me but soon stopped.

I felt that the ground slipped from under my feet.

"But Robin I really didn't know she is Charulata." I tried to soothe him but he gripped my collar and warned me to leave. Rahul came in between and persuaded me to go back to the hostel. I left the party which was no more a party and came back. I had thought that I would go to sleep with good memories of the evening but it had become a nightmare, as my mind was on Robin. My mobile rang. It was Rahul informing me that Robin would be staying with him for the night. The whole night just passed just tossing and turning on my bed. I was worried about my estrangement with Robin for something which was not intentional.

Next day several times I tried to break the ice with Robin but he avoided me whenever I approached him. A few days later, I was in the laboratory for my biochem practicals. Robin was my partner for preparing the assignment.    He asked the professor to assign him with someone else but the professor refused. So he went to the other groups and hung out with them. I felt utterly humiliated. Rahul could sense my feelings as on many occasions I was on the verge of tears. After class I went to the library as I was all alone. I saw Rahul with Robin move towards the canteen with some other guys. These were the same guys who always incited Robin. Robin looked very unhappy and sad was every now and then looking at the canteen doorway.

"What happened Robin? You look edgy," Rahul asked.

"No... Why? I am all right," he replied.

"Then who are you looking for to see at the door?" Rahul asked.

"Why? No one," he replied.

"Don't you miss Raj?" Rahul asked suddenly.

"Don't take that bastard's name in front of me…….. I hate him," Robin said angrily, his face turning red.

"You lying, I know you are missing Raj here," Rahul said.

"Shut up... I don't miss any one. If you miss him, you go to him," Robin shouted.

"Why should Robin miss Raj? He is not worth missing," one of the guys said.

"What hasn't Robin done for Raj, but that dirty bloody bastard deceived his friend," another incited.

"You people keep quiet, it is our personal affair. And even Raj has done a lot for Robin and me," Rahul admonished them.

"What has he done for me? He flirted with his friend's girl and disgraced his friendship. He tried to take away a Rajput's girl, which he doesn't know is impossible," Robin raged.

"Is she your girl? Does she love you? Have you proposed to her?" Rahul asked.

Robin kept quiet.

"Raj is a betrayer. A person who cheated his best friend will fuck and leave the girl," one of the guys said.

Robin's face was now turning red and his facial muscles were visibly contracting.

"He is just a motherfu…" the same tried to add but before he could complete the sentence Robin punched his face hard.

"You bastard! You are abusing my friend in front of me?" Robin stood up and shouted.

"Don't you dare and abuse my friend! What he is or is not I know better than you guys, get lost you *benchod*," he warned.

At once the guys left the table and went to the other end of the canteen.

"Robin, you love Raj, I always knew it," Rahul said.

"Shut up… I don't care for that rascal," Robin shouted.

"I am not like him. I can't disgrace my friendship. I can't bear to hear bad words about him," Robin said.

"Raj did not know that girl was Charulata, Robin. I know Raj committed a mistake but it was not intentional, I bet he could not have hurt you intentionally," Rahul said.

"He has already hurt me a lot and stop advocating for him."

After a week we had our submissions. As Robin was not with me so he hadn't prepared any report. Every body submitted their work. Robin was standing at the other end looking elsewhere. I quickly wrote down Robin's name on my report and submitted it to our professor. After two days the marks for the assignment was put up on the notice board. Someone informed Robin that he had got full marks. Robin at once rushed to the notice board and when he saw his marks was utterly surprised.

"Hey Rahul, I got full marks though I had not submitted my paper," Robin said.

"See my charm? This is what is called Rajput shaan," he said touching his collar.

"Have you seen Raj's marks?" Rahul asked.

"What have I to do with his marks? I am not interested," Robin shrugged.

"You must see it in order to know the secret behind your marks," Rahul said.

Robin once again viewed all the names and found my name and the marks written against it.

"Raj has got zero! How is it possible?" Robin said in wonderment.

"Possible dear as he submitted his own paper putting your name on it," Rahul said stroking Robin's shoulders. "This is called friendship and not your so-called Rajput shaan."

"That fucker has once again hurt my ego, perhaps he feels good doing it," Robin said.

"What's your problem? If he unintentionally commits a mistake it's bad and if he intentionally does something good, again bad," Rahul said sounding irritated.

"I don't need his pity. I didn't work so I don't deserve any marks. He knows very well I hate it if someone shows any sort of pity on me. But yet he did this," Robin said.

"I don't know why you are so negative about him. Charu is yours, he will never meet her again but at least you should talk to him. You are punishing him for a mistake which he didn't commit intentionally," Rahul said.

"I again tell you and you can make him understand too, I never accept anything second hand, not even my love. He may carry on with Charu but never mention her name in front of me," he said.

"This is your problem. Why are you so egoistic? Why do you put your Rajput shaan everywhere? You will face a big problem if you will not resolve this problem of yours. .How can you be so selfish? You think only of yourself, have you ever thought about Raj's sufferings?" Rahul said with irritation.

"Friendship is a relationship of forgiveness and sacrifice. You can flaunt your pride everywhere but you can't understand this simple thing," Rahul said.

Rahul's words worked and they came to me in the library. Rahul tried to mediate, we hugged each other but due to a month's rift conversation was a bit stilted. It took a week for us to become normal again. I avoided Charu and her discussion not only in front of Robin but anywhere. Several times I changed my path when I saw her from a distance. Sometimes when it became unbearable I used to shed tears in private. I tell you it is very difficult to kill one's love. But Robin was more important to me.

# Shivani & her office: A look

"Shivani…. Shivani….. Get up. You know the time?"

"Shivani…. Its really very late beta… get up. Don't you have to go to office today?"

"Ya mom…. But I can't force my eyes open," groaned Shivani.

"Enough sleeping for today. Get ready or you will get late. Don't you have to appear before your Asst. manager?"

On hearing the last bit Shivani instantaneously leapt out of her bed.  She sprinted towards the bathroom and within twenty minutes she was all ready and sitting at the breakfast table.

"Mom… please pack my tiffin."

"Ya I am packing it. Would you like some pickles?"

"Whatever mom, but please, fast."

"I am not late Shivani, you are late. Here, take your tiffin."

Shivani collected it and ran out of the door.

"Shivani….you didn't have your breakfast?"

"Mom I don't have time. I am already late."

Bye kittu, bye mom. She ran out of the gate and instantly collided against a scooter standing in the street.

"Munirka is such a bloody congested place," she cursed.

She was wearing a green salwar kameez. The time was half past eight. It was the time which used to be a mood freshener for all the young boys including teenage boys of Munirka. Shivani's elegance used to be soothing for their eyes to see the first thing in the morning. Even late risers started getting up early to have a glimpse of her.

Just nineteen years old she was a fun loving, helping, cheerful, innocent and of course the most beautiful girl of Munirka. Her untied wet hair was kissing her waist.

She saw her watch and screamed, "Oh my God… it's going to be 8.45 and I am still so far from Munirka bus stand."

Again she ran into something. This time it was not a scooter but a young man.

"Hell…. What's happening today?" she said in irritation.

The collision was powerful and the muddy street of Munirka would have kissed her glass- like body had not a strong hand came between them and held Shivani. In between that her pink bag escaped from her hand and thank God it got a safe place on a scooter's handle. Even scooters can be kind sometimes.

Shivani opened her eyes and saw the person holding her and again closed her eyes. Suddenly her mobile rang. She was in another world.

"Your mobile is ringing." The young man said giving her a shake.

"O ya…"

As she stood up on her feet her dupatta slipped from her shoulders. Again the same hand caught it before it kissed the moist ground and draped it back on her shoulders.

"Be careful," he said.

Shivani was on the phone so she couldn't answer him.

"Hello…"

"Hello madam, where are you? We are waiting for you near the bus stand. We are getting late."

"Ya Ramesh bhaia, I am just reaching. I am not far. In five minutes I will be there."

"Come soon, bye." The phone hung up.

"Rahul…. you…? How you move in the street? Couldn't you see a 5 foot 7 inch beautiful girl?"

"O ….. P.T Usha, I was not running absent mindedly in this congested street, and for your kind information you collided with me and not me with you," young man replied aggressively.

"Oh, very funny…. If you were mindful then you could have stopped this collision," she chuckled.

There was really a point there and poor Rahul became answerless.

Yes, he is the same Rahul, a medico and the best friend of mine and Robin.

"I think you are going to office and you are already late. Aren't you?" Rahul reminded her.

"Oh ya… I have to go now and that's why I am sparing you," she said pointing her index finger at Rahul.

She again started running. Rahul and Shivani went in opposite directions.

"Really this is ridiculous. People have just forgotten words like sorry and thank you. I stopped her from getting muddy and she is fighting with me," Rahul grumbled to himself.

"O God you made my day. Thank you very much. Now I don't care about Asst Manager or anyone." Shivani chirped.

The two different emotions were at opposite directions but it was so pure and innocent that it was spreading fragrance.

"Sorry Ramesh bhaia I got late. Actually, I…."

"Explain it to the manager later Shivani, Now get into the cab, we are already very late."

Shivani used to catch her office cab from here. Actually her company provided door to door facility but it was difficult even for a small cab to enter Munirka's congested street where half the street was occupied with people living on both the sides. Some of them used to even cook and even wash their clothes here.

The population of India is growing with maximum speed. Most of the people in Munirka live in small house and their members are increasing. In front of almost every house you will see a scooter. These scooters have their own story. At least three generations live in a small house. The third generation belongs to kids. This generation doesn't have any problem as most of the time they are out of the house. After school they have their lunch and immediately after that they go out to play. Rests of the two generations are problematic to each other. Son and father at the same time can't be inside the house as the architecture of house does not allow much privacy. So when the first generation is inside the second generation makes their arsis comfortable on these scooters. I am really worried for both the population rise and the latest use of scooters.

"You are looking gorgeous today Shivani," a colleague complimented.

"Thanks Nilesh," Shivani said without showing any expression.

"Shivani, can we have lunch together today?" asked Nilesh.

"No thanks Nilesh, today I am carrying my lunch."

"What you are doing today evening?" Nilesh asked again.

"If you don't mind can we go for a movie?"

"Stop flirting Nilesh. I am really not interested," finally she lost her temper.

Nilesh could not say anything after that.

After a 40 minute drive they were in Okhla Phase III. The cab stopped near a magnificent building. Exhibition Today Pvt. Ltd 279 – B.

As the car stopped Shivani's heart beat became faster. She took her usual seat and switched on her computer.

Shivani worked for Exhibition Today as a data centre executive. This company organizes exhibitions for prestigious firms. It had a great name in this field as they could arrange any type of exhibitions. Many national and international companies were their clients.

Shivani was perspiring in the AC chamber.

"Here, have a glass of water," Rashmi offered a glass to Shivani.

"Thanks Rashmi. Today because of me all the other guys are late."

"Ya, I know. Your cab driver had already reported it to Asst manager Kanut."

"Ya I know yaar, I am waiting for his call," Shivani said fearfully.

A peon came to Shivani and said, "Madam, Mr. Kanut is calling you."

"Ok, tell him I am coming."

Approaching the cabin, Shivani said, "May I come in Sir?"

Kanut was busy on the phone. His cabin was made of glass. He gestured to wait.

She was standing in front of Kanut's chamber. It was making her a bit upset as many staff members were staring at her.

Kanut took at least ten minutes on the phone and then called Shivani in.

Kanut was in his late thirties with thick, curly hair, well dressed but big and bulging eyes like a frog in a horror film. One thing which was known to every body about Kanut was his weakness for women. He in fact deserved the title 'Womanizer of the century'.

"Ya Miss Shivani Kashyap how are you today?"

"I am fine sir. How are you?" she replied with a pale face.

"I am always fine Shivani but late comers make me uncomfortable."

"Sir, actually I slipped and fell down in the street and my clothes got dirty so I had to change and in this process I got late," explained Shivani.

"Oh I see…. I always tell you to walk carefully as in youthful days steps are unbalanced usually."

"By the way, why don't you make some unbalanced move in my office? You and I both will be benefited with that." He said putting his hand under the table.

"I don't get you, sir," Shivani said with a red face

"You don't understand, that's the real problem baby. I think one day you will get what I am saying. Now go back to your work and remember don't be late again."

Shivani turned to go back when suddenly Kanut said, "By the way you are looking damn sexy today Shivani."

Shivani didn't pay any attention and came back to her seat.

"What was Kanut saying?" Rashmi asked.

"What else except his double meaning rubbish?" Shivani replied.

"I don't know why all guys look at women as though they were spicy chicken flesh?" Shivani said in disgust. He is also a guy but he never looks at me like others do. Only he has the right to look at me with that kind of eyes but he doesn't do so, "she said with a helpless face.

"Who is this guy, madam? You never told me about him," Rashmi said nudging Shivani's arm with her elbows

"He is my childhood friend Rahul Tyagi."

"Childhood friend…..? Still you are not in a relationship?" asked Rashmi.

"No, we are not in a relationship Rashmi but still it is a beautiful and strong bond."

"Have you ever expressed your feelings to him?"

"Not directly but indirectly several times," replied Shivani.

"What do you think? Rahul loves you?"

"I know he loves me." Shivani said with great confidence.

"How can you say it with so much confidence?"

"I love him since I was nine years old and I never got the same feeling for any other guy. If I can love him like that I am pretty sure he is in love with me too". Shivani said with a sigh.

"Shh…Kanut is coming Rashmi….."

Soon Rashmi and Shivani took their position in front of their respective computers.

"What you are doing Shivani?" Kanut asked.

"Sir I am correcting the data of mobile service provider companies."

"Shivani, I hope you know that your target is to correct the data of at least a hundred companies in a day, so work properly," Kanut commanded.

"And what about you Rashmi?"

"Sir I am making calls for our new exhibition Global convergence"

"Be fast ladies, we should have at least 200 paid delegates," Kanut said scratching his head.

"Shivani from tomorrow you will make calls for delegates, and after lunch we will seat for a brief training in the conference room. Is it ok for you?"

"Yes sir". Shivani replied.

Kanut went away.

"Shivani… this man is a real bastard. He doesn't work at all and gets a handsome salary". Rashmi said with anger.

"Yaar, he is lucky he has been appointed for commanding us". Shivani said.

"Be careful. He will sit for one hour with you and half of it he will pass flirting with you". Rashmi warned.

"I know his penis is a trouble for him," Shivani said laughing.

It is half past one. Lunch time.

"Shivani... It is time to have lunch," Rashmi reminded Shivani.

All the staffs of the data center were having their lunch. People exchanged their special recipe with each other. Rashmi and Shivani always shared their tiffin. They were limited to each other.  Half an hour of lunch used to be a good time for all of the staffs. Shivani and Rashmi used to go out for a one rupee chocolate after having their lunch. That one rupee chocolate was their dessert.

A handicapped old man used to sit under the shadow of a big tree. He was surrounded with a ball, half a loaf of bread, a piece of pickle and a half liter water bottle. When passing him Shivani uses to give the old man a 5 rupee coin every day.

"I see you give this old man a coin daily. Why you do so?"

"I do this because of two reasons. First I want to help this old handicapped man with whatever small way I can help him, and second by helping this man I get a chance to pray to god O God, please make me meet my love soon."

"You are really mad Shivani," Rashmi said laughing.

Sharp at two pm, they had to be at their desk. After half an hour Shivani got a call from Kanut to join him in the conference room.

"May I come in sir?"

"Ya Shivani, come in, make yourself comfortable".

It was a large room with a seating capacity for thirty people. On a big table one laptop was placed facing Kanut.

"Sit next to me Shivani. Why are you are sitting so far?"

Shivani took the seat next to Kanut.

"It's a simple training so don't be tensed".

"I am not tensed because of training but because of your rascality" Shivani thought to herself.

"No… sir…. I am alright".

"Ok tell me Shivani, what is the secret of your excellent figure?"

This bastard has started again thought Shivani. She did not reply. She kept her head bent down.

"You were looking gorgeous in untied wet hairs in the morning. Has anyone ever told you that your lips are like rose petals?"

"No sir. I don't think anyone looks me as keenly as you do." Shivani said shortly

Suddenly Mrs. Sunita Vats, the manager of data center, entered the conference room.

Instantly Kanut changed his tone.

"So as I was telling you about ICT industry. ICT stands for information communication technology…....." and pretended as he was doing his job perfectly.

"How was your training Shivani?" Rashmi asked later.

"Thanks God Sunita maam came, otherwise that rascal had decided to fuck my mind".

"What was he saying?"

"What else except figure, sex, beauty and other damn things".

It was now 6 pm. The staff started filling their log book which used to be the manual report of what an individual had done that day. It used to be checked by Kanut and Sunita.

People started to board their respective cabs but unfortunately the cabs in which Rashmi and Shivani went were still on the way. Rashmi lived in Uttam Nagar.

# Tale of an innocent Love: Part I

"What to do now Rashmi, our cabs are late?" Shivani groaned.

There was a security personnel; she inquired how much time the cabs would take to come.

"Rashmi, it will take at least 30 minutes," Shivani informed Rashmi.

"What do we till then, yaar?" Shivani again asked.

Rashmi thought a while and said, "Ok, I have an idea. Tell me about Rahul and how you met him etc."

Do you really want to know?" Shivani asked.

"Ya, of course yaar". Rashmi replied enthusiastically.

"Ok I will tell you about the day when I first met Rahul".

"Ya, that will be better" Rashmi said

"First I would like to say that we both are from the same colony Munirka. His house is not very far from mine. His father was a teacher in Rose Mary public school in which I was studying. Rahul took admission in that school in standard IV. Before that he was staying with his grand father in Haryana. Since childhood he is very shy. I still remember his first day in school. He didn't talk a single word with any one. I don't know why but I was attracted to him since day one. Next day we learnt that he was a very intelligent student. One day I saw him near a shop. I was with my friend Madhu who was older than me. I asked Madhu "Who is that guy? Does he live in this colony?"

"Ya he lives in this colony and his name is Rahul," Madhu said.

"I know he is Rahul but I did not know he lives here as I have never seen him earlier?"

"He is in my class, a very shy guy" I added.

"Ya, he is very shy and he came here just a week back. Before that he was staying with our grand father," Madhu said.

"Our grandfather?"

"Yah, he is my brother" Madhu added.

I was shocked. "Your brother!!"

The world is really small. Generally in the evenings we used to gather at Madhu's house to play games in the "gali". I used to see Rahul sitting and studying his course books. He was unlike other guys. Perhaps he was solitude -loving person.

"I would like to know something about Madhu," Rashmi interrupted. "Wasn't Madhu with you guys in school?"

"Earlier she was but she left school as she was suffering from epilepsy ...a sort of mental disorder," Shivani explained.

"That's why we used to gather at her house so that she could play with us. She is a very sweet girl and my best friend" she further added.

One day I asked Madhu, "Why doesn't your brother play with us?"

"He is not interested in games," she said.

"Ask him to join us, he sits all alone, I feel bad for him," I said

"Rahul come join us, we are playing an interesting game," Madhu said to Rahul.

"No Di, I don't want to play, I am fine here," he gave a dry reply.

But after several requests by Madhu he joined us. We usually used to play bride and groom. For selection of the bride and groom we used to do lucky draw separately for the bride and the groom. I was chosen the bride of the evening for the first time ever. Then the lucky draw for the groom was done and to my surprise Rahul became my first ever groom. Rest of the kids were divided as barati sharati. Madhu was playing the character of the groom's sis. We were children so we definitely were not aware of each and every custom of marriage but we did our level best to give it an original touch. You know Rashmi, that day Rahul put vermilion on my head. I can never forget that special day of my life. Once I had seen a groom kissing his bride in an English film but Rahul was not kissing me and no one was suggesting him to do so even. So after waiting 5 minutes I myself kissed Rahul on his lips. Every one was stunned.

"You kissed Rahul on the lips! You are crazy, man!" Rashmi laughed.

"Ya I kissed him but I paid a lot for that," Shivani said.

"How?" Rashmi asked.

"Rahul never came to play with us after that," Shivani said with pain.

"But how and how dare you kiss him yaar?"

"I don't know really, suddenly I lost control and our lips became one for a while," Shivani reminisced dreamily.

"That evening I couldn't do any thing, I was restless and Rahul's face was dancing before my eyes," she added.

That day I asked my mother, "Mom, what is marriage?"

Mom explained, "Marriage is a pious bond between two persons — one of them is a man and other a woman. It is a promise to share each others' every happiness and sorrow and to cooperate with each other at every step of life. Husband becomes the first priority of a woman. In other words he is supposed to be the master or God for the woman. Apart of all these facts last but not the least marriage happens once in a life time."

"Mom's these few lines became powerful determination of my life and even today it guides me. From that day onwards I consider Rahul as my husband."

"Are you crazy Shivani, it was merely a game and was not real," Rashmi said.

"For me that game became my biggest dream, Rashmi. Perhaps you will understand my feeling but the truth is that I belong to Rahul both mentally and physically."

Two cars enter in the premises and security came and informed them.

"Shivani your love story is amazing. I would love to hear each and every thing," Rashmi said.

"Ya sure, any time," Shivani said with a smile.

# Ajab Pyar Ki Gajab Chemistry

It was 7 in the evening when Shivani got off from her office cab at Munirka bus stand. It was really a beautiful misty evening, the shops around were looking impressive with colorful lights. A soft wind was blowing bringing with it the mixed fragrance of sweets and spices. Shivani's mouth started to water from those fragrances. She was looking around. Suddenly her face started glowing. A few guys were standing near Agarwal's Sweet Corner. Suddenly she went there and asked one of them, "Excuse me Mr. Correct me if I am wrong but aren't you the guy because of whom I got late to office today and had to hear a lot of rubbish from my Asst Manager?"

The tall well built man turned around. It was Rahul.

"What is this joke Shivani?" Rahul asked.

"For you it may be a joke but I know how much I suffered" she said a bit loudly.

Rahul managed to take away Shivani a little far from his friends and said, "What do you want?"

"Every thing but for now I want you to give me a treat" she said mischievously.

"No it's not possible as I am standing with my friends. What will they think?" he said looking towards his friends.

"Let them think whatever, I don't care. But I felt good that you think that much about me" she said with pushing a few strands of hair behind her ear.

"Either you give me treat or I will hold your hand publicly," she threatened mischievously.

"I don't have any money" Rahul said with an angry face.

"You give me a treat, I will pay the bill. Tum bhi kya yaad rakhoge kisi raish se paala pada tha" she said with gesture.

She moved forward to hold his hands, at once Rahul agreed to give her a treat. They went towards Agarwal Sweets.

"What would like to have, Rani Jee?" he asked.

"I don't want to have anything here. Stuff here are very costly and not that good, so let's go to some other shop," she suggested.

They went to a small shop where samosa and chaat were available.

"Now tell me what you would like to have?" Rahul asked.

"Two samosas only," she said.

"Bhaia two samosas please" ordered Rahul.

"Why only two samosas? Won't you have any thing?" she asked.

"No I wouldn't." he said.

"Ok then I also don't want to have anything" she said with low pitch.

"Why Shivani? It's not fair. You wanted a treat that's why we came here" Rahul said angrily.

"If you won't take anything then I also don't want any thing and by the way I am very hungry," she said and looked obliquely at Rahul.

"You are too much Shivani ! Really impossible. Two more samosas bhaia."

Shivani was having her samosa and she got a golden chance to look at Rahul. Rahul was sitting silently with his head bent down. Shivani was smiling. After having the samosas Shivani pulled out her wallet from her bag but by then Rahul had paid bill. She again smiled.

"Won't you give me company till home?" asked Shivani.

"No……. you go on your own."

"Ok ok, don't show so much attitude, I am going," she turned towards her home.

"Excuse me, Miss Shivani. Perhaps you have completely forgotten the word thanks and sorry?" Rahul reminded.

"But why should I say sorry and thanks?" she asked with a question mark on her face.

"You should say thanks because I have just given you a treat and sorry because in the morning you collided with me," he reminded.

"Ha ha… you really think so? You had to give the treat as because of you I got late to office so no matter of thanks and you collided with me and not me with you. You should have seen a beautiful girl struggling to make her way through a congested street. So there's no question of saying sorry. In fact you should be sorry," she finished.

"No one can win in a discussion with you, you better go," Rahul said with folded hands.

"Ya, no one can. But you can sweetheart," she mumbled and went.

Shivani reached home.

"Mom, di has come," Kittu said.

"Shivani why are you so late?" her mother asked.

"Mom, today my cab was late so I came late and as I was hungry I ate Chaat on the way and so got late," she explained.

"I was really worried beta."

"Kittu did you gone to school today?" Shivani asked.

"Of cores di… and I didn't come late like you. Where were you?" Kittu asked in an elder brother fashion.

"Just because I am your younger brother doesn't mean I will not ask you where you been," Kittu said expanding his chest.

"Oh so you have become very old now," Shivani said pulling Kittu's cheeks.

"Mom what's there for dinner?" Shivani asked.

"Your favorite chicken biryani darling," mom said stroking Shivani's head.

"I thought your mood must be off due to your Asst manager, so I thought Biryani will put some smile back on your beautiful face," mom added.

Shivani held her from the back and said, "You are the best mom in this world."

"Mom let me prepare some tomato chutney," she said and started choosing tomatoes for it.

She started making chutney while humming a hit song from DDLG, which is a favorite song of every young girl, "Mere khwabo me Jo aaye".

Her mom came to her and said, "You look very happy today?"

"Ya I am happy as my mom has prepared my favorite dish," she said hugging her mother.

"It may be one of the reasons of your good mood but what is the main reason for you to make tomato chutney?" asked mom.

"Should I tell you the truth mom?" Shivani said.

"Ya of course as I have all rights to know," mom said.

"Mom today morning I met Rahul and in the evening he gave me a treat," she said happily.

"Actually I forced him to give me a treat," she said.

"Why did you force him to give a treat?"

"Today I was already late so I was running and in my hurry I collided with him in the street and then I myself started a war of words with him and in the evening I told him that I became late just because of him, so give me a treat as my boss scolded me very much," she said mischievously.

"You really are very naughty Shivani," her mom said caressing her hairs.

"You know mom, he is very shy and sadly he doesn't care to spend even a minute with me," she said hopelessly.

"He is a very shy guy, Shivani so he is uncomfortable with girls," her mom said.

"I hope there is no other reason for his discomfort," she said mischievously.

"What could be another reason?" mom asked anxiously.

"Who knows he may be a gay ha ha ha…" she chirped.

"What rubbish, you shouldn't say such for a guy like him," mom laughed and went.

"Mom chutney is ready. I am very hungry. Come, we will have dinner together."

"Kittu…. Kittu….. Oh where's he gone?"

"O God!he slept off again . This boy is impossible!"

"Kittu get up, have your dinner."

Now the three members of small family were on the dining table with their usual discussion of how they spent the day. It was now 11 pm. Shivani went to bed. She was recalling every moment which she passed with Rahul. The moments with him were very few and short but these were her life's best moments. It was her daily routine to remember them.

"I don't know what the person is doing of whom I think several times a day? Does he remember me even once a day?" several such questions arose in her mind.

Today Rahul was a bit restless on bed. As he closed his eyes Shivani's beautiful face floated before him. He at once opened his eyes. Again he closed his eyes and the same thing happened.

"Why is Shivani face coming before me when I close my eyes?"

"Perhaps because I met her twice today," he answered his question himself.

"Why does this gal make me uncomfortable since childhood I don't know!"

The scene of his collision with Shivani in the morning was repeatedly dancing before his eyes. Both Shivani and he were changing their sides on their respective beds continuously. This is the magic of love which does not let one go to sleep so easily. I know it because I was putting up at Rahul's house and Shivani sometimes used to visit his house.

# A Tale of innocent Love: Part II

Next morning was very fresh for Rahul. He was a meritorious student and he had cracked the PMT exam but economically he was not sound. He didn't attend the lecture. During lunch Robin and I went to the cafeteria to have lunch, there I saw Rahul sitting totally depressed. We went near him. Having seen us he tried to be normal but his uneasiness could be easily read.

"What happened Rahul"? Robin asked.

"Nothing," he replied.

"You didn't turn up for lecture and now you are hiding something," I asked.

"You know Raj… what's the condition of my house," he reluctantly said. "Nothing is hidden from you."

"You know papa took loan for Madhu's marriage as the demand of the guy was very high," he added.

"Why did you people then spoil her life by tying her knot with such a greedy man?" Robin asked.

"Madhu was not normal she was epileptic. No one was ready to marry her."

"She got married when she was only seventeen to a man who was thirty years old at that time."

"I couldn't do anything as I myself was 12 years old but one thing is clear I hate my brother -in -law the most" he said with a red face.

We had our lunch and again went back to the lab for Biochem practicals.

Sitting in her office Shivani was scratching her head on the new project of convincing delegates to attend the exhibition.

It was lunch time. As usual they finished their lunch and went out, bought chocolate and Shivani gave that old man a 5 rupee coin and closed her eyes for a few seconds.

"Praying for your love again?" asked Rashmi.

Shivani nodded her head and smiled.

"Whenever I see a smile and confidence on your face, I always think one thing about Rahul..... How lucky he is?" Rashmi said.

"That day you had not narrated your entire love story so finish it now as there's still some time." Rashmi implored.

"Where were we?" asked Shivani.

"You kissed Rahul and after that Rahul did not play with you," Rashmi reminded.

"Did you get a chance to meet Rahul again?" Rashmi asked.

"I used to meet him daily in class but we never talked. But I used to go his house every day to meet Madhu."

I will tell you a memorable incident of my life which is related to Rahul. We were a bit young then. I think I was 13. It was afternoon and I was returning from school on my bicycle. Not very far from my house, my skirt got caught in the rims of the bicycle's wheel. I fell down and grazed my knees badly. I got up and tried to pull my skirt out of the spokes but it had got entangled badly. I tried in vain to pull it out but it was not coming out and it started tearing. Many people went by but no one came forward to help me. Some even whistled as they went past me and a few even winked. Thank God Rahul saw me and ran towards me and tried his best to extricate my skirt from the spokes but all attempts were in vain. My skirt had got badly torn by then and a portion of my right thigh became visible to the thirsty eyes of a few bastards standing there. Rahul quickly took off his shirt and offered it to me and said "tie it around your waist."

I didn't ask any thing and did accordingly. He then pulled out my skirt from the spokes with a force. It came out but was completely torn. Thanks to his shirt which saved my dignity. I was delighted with his gallantry. Mom became very upset after seeing me like that. I narrated the entire episode to her. I could see a bundle of thanks in my mom's eyes for Rahul. I removed his shirt from my waist and looked at it lovingly but after a few minutes I became bashful. For the very first time I felt some sort of quiver in my body. I started kissing his shirt and even wore it and slept wearing it for a few hours. Mom pressed it and I went his house to return it.

"Now I will tell you the most important thing which happened that day." she said with a sense of modesty.

"What happened?" Rashmi asked curiously.

"That day I got my first periods," she said bashfully.

"You mean you got your first menses?" Rashmi asked.

She nodded with a smile.

This is how Shivani stepped into her youth. There was undoubtedly a great love which was smoldering in her heart.

Sometimes Shivani used to visit our medical college especially on Saturdays when she used to be free as she used to work five days a week.

I knew Shivani but we had never spoken. Last year on Rakshabandhan, she visited Rahul's house as Madhu had come to tie Rakhi on her brother's wrist. It was August end and I was very busy with my 1st year exams. In the evening when I returned I met Madhu and Shivani.

At once Shivani asked "Why is your wrist without any Rakhi bhaiya?"

"This is because I don't have sister" while saying this I became a little emotional.

"I know this is a filmy dialogue but then I am saying, who says you don't have a sis? I am like your sis and if you don't mind can I tie rakhi on my brother's wrist?" she said it with comedy but lastly got emotional.

She and Madhu tied rakhi on my wrist and it was a beginning of a sweet relationship which I had not felt till then. When I tried to offer money to my sisters, they in unity refused it and then I don't know consciously or unconsciously I made a commitment before everyone that when my sisters will be in any trouble or when they will need me I will do anything for them even if I have to risk my life.

That day I knew one thing about human behavior; it becomes really emotional and makes promises or commitments when it gets anything which he had never thought. Perhaps this new relationship was like that.

No doubt she used to visit our college with some excuse or the other; sometimes I used to be her excuse as she can't reveal even before me that she was missing Rahul so couldn't stopped herself from visiting our college. She was very frank with me but as an ideal sister she always respected the relationship which we used to share. She never said anything about her love for Rahul.

One such Saturday she came during lunch break when I, Rahul and Robin were having our lunch in college's canteen. We trio used to have our lunch together.

"Hey Shivani... how did you remember your brother today?" I asked.

When Rahul saw Shivani, he became somewhat upset.

"What happened to you Rahul?" Robin asked.

He didn't answer but I too noticed that day for that very first time that Shivani's presence used to upset him.

"Nothing like that bhaiya actually I was getting bored and also we had not met for long, so I thought better to visit my brother. Can't I come to see you?" she asked.

"Why not Shivani... now you have here two brothers instead of one," Robin said.

I and Robin were sometimes alike regarding emotions. We both had no sister of our own but now we had a common sister that's Shivani.

# My Introduction with divine hidden love

No doubt Robin had a great love for Shivani. We passed our time for a whole hour then we had to go for Physiology practicals which used to be very boring.

After class we came to our room and I saw Robin looking very restless.

"What's eating you up?" I asked.

"Ya... I think yes there is something."

"Did you ever notice Rahul becomes upset and behaves complete differently when Shivani is here?" he added.

"Ya... you are right, today first time I noticed it," I replied with a mixed feeling.

"Did you ever notice Shivani's eyes, which wants to say something?" he asked.

"What her eyes want to say and what is this all about? Is this a puzzle?"

"I think so... I mean this is no less than a puzzle" Robin said scratching his head.

"Will you just elaborate your point?" I asked.

"Raj, I think Shivani loves Rahul and yet nothing is happening in that direction because Rahul is not responding," he explained.

"How do you know and on what basis you discovered it?" I again asked.

"I don't know whether you have noticed or not but Shivani was indirectly commenting on Rahul and while talking she was constantly looking at Rahul, forgetting that she was talking to us," he tried to substantiate his statement.

I felt as Robin was very much right.

In bed at night I made my mind I must find out more fishy case of Shivani and Rahul. After a couple of days I got a call from Shivani on my mobile.

"Bhaiya...today you and Robin bhaiya will have dinner at my house"

"Is there any good news?" I asked.

"Come and you will come to know" she replied.

"Ok we will be there today for dinner," I confirmed.

"Bhaiya do me a favor... I have called Rahul too, but he may not come, so please ask him to come along with you," she requested.

I didn't know what was the dinner for? But I was sure today I will definitely ask Shivani about Rahul. Robin and I were in canteen for lunch.

"Robin did you get a call from Shivani?" I asked

"Ya... she asked us to come to her house for dinner along with Rahul," he replied.

"I think this is the best time to ask Shivani about Rahul" I said.

"Yes... ask her if everything is alright or not," he suggested.

Rahul too came and joined us.

"What's up buddy?" he greeted us.

"All fine Rahul... Where are you now a day's man? At least call us sometimes," Robin complained.

"Actually I was busy in preparing assignments with Mohit" he said.

"What's special today?" I asked Rahul.

"What's the date?" he asked.

"19th December" Robin said.

"Shivani's birthday!!!!" Rahul said

"Shivani's birthday??" I and Robin said in unison.

"How you know?" again we asked in unison.

"I don't know I just guessed as her birth month is December," he said lamely.

"She has invited us to come to her house today," I said.

"Go...enjoy the party..." he said.

"What do you mean go? You too will come with us," Robin said.

"No yaar... not possible," he said refusing.

"But we have promised her that you too will come with us," I said.

"But I..." I interrupted him

"Robin is a Rajput and he has already promised Shivani which means you are coming as it's a matter of Rajpooti promise which can't fail" I said and looked at Robin. I tried to incite Robin. I guess it was enough. Rahul was looking at me as I am putting him before Robin's Rajput pride.

"Yes...Definitely a Rajput's promise can't fail," confirmed Robin.

I was happy that my plan executed well. All excuses of Rahul were rubbished by Robin and after a few minutes Rahul too realized that it was useless to convince a Rajput like Robin after such a provocation.

"You will have to help us to buy a few gifts for Shivani," Robin said.

"Ok... I will do whatever you will ask as you are not ready to listen to anything," he condescended irritatingly.

"Let's meet at Priya at 7 o' clock in the evening," I said.

"Ok give me a call when you both reach Priya," Rahul said.

We all met there at time.

Now choosing a gift was a problem.

"Rahul you are Shivani's childhood friend, you must be knowing what she likes?" Robin said.

"I am her friend but I don't know her," he said.

We were all confused what to choose? Choosing a gift for a girl sometimes sucks.

At last Rahul said "Gift her teddy bear... she may love it."

At once we made up our mind to buy a teddy in order to set our mind free of these stupid gifts.

"I am just coming, you pay your bill" Rahul said and went somewhere.

When we came out we saw Rahul sitting on his bike. We all departed for Shivani's house on our bikes.

We knocked the door. Shivani opened the door and greeted us with a smile but when she saw Rahul her happiness was evident.

"Thanks for coming bhaiya," she said holding me and Robin.

"Thank you very much for bringing along this idiot," she said pointing to Rahul.

We presented the gift to Shivani.

"What's in it bhaiya?" she said being inquisitive.

"This is my sister's birthday gift" Robin said caressing her head.

"How did you know it is my birthday today?" she asked.

"Rahul told us," I said.

"Such a scoundrel…" she murmured and looked at Rahul.

There was no more surprise so she thought to cut the cake. It was a small family party with no more ten friends of Shivani. Her brother Kittu offered us cake and other eatables. I was noticing Shivani as she was a bit restless. She was searching for something among the gifts which she had got. Finally she brought out a gift item packed wrapped in pink paper with a smile and expression which was a proof of her satisfaction. She smelled it deep and kept near her heart for a few minutes. She was unaware that a pair of eyes was looking at her. She went in her room with that gift and came back soon holding a saucer full of cakes. She offered us cake and moved towards Rahul. Her hand trembled a little in front of Rahul but at once Rahul's hand came in support of hers. He took a piece of cake. Their fingers touched each others beneath the saucer.

"I am leaving now," Rahul said.

"Why buddy?" Robin asked.

"Mom has already prepared my dinner…" Rahul said.

"Cant you stay some more?" Shivani pleaded.

Rahul didn't say anything and sat down. I was really happy that anyway Rahul did care about Shivani.

"Dinner will be served soon," Shivani said.

She went to talk to her friends and I noticed she was secretly looking at Rahul now and then. I couldn't stop myself.

I came to shivani and said "Shivani I need to talk to you."

"Ya... sure bhaia."

"Not here...Somewhere else," I said.

She looked at me inquisitively and said, "Come to my room."

I looked at Robin and he understood my mission.

"Tell me bhaia... Is everything alright?" she asked.

"That I want to know Shivani" I said.

"I didn't get you," she said with a blank face.

"I want to know is everything alright between you and Rahul?" I asked.

"Yes everything is alright bhaia, But why are you asking this?" she said.

"I am asking because I guess there is something which is eating my sister from inside, I am not only your brother but also your friend," I said.

She sighed and said "Bhaia I also wanted to tell you and Robin bhaia but the relationship we share didn't permit me."

"I am proud of you Shivani but I can't bear to see you like this, so tell me everything," I said.

"Bhaiya... I... I...don't know how to say it?"

"You love him?" I asked at once as I could guess what was happening to her.

"Yes bhaiya... very much," she said and turned back.

She narrated me whole story which she had narrated to Rashmi but in short.

I caressed her head and lifted her head which was tilted downward with bashfulness.

"Why you never told him?" I asked.

"How can I? He always avoids me and above all I am a girl," she explained.

"I know he loves me too but I don't know why he never tells me his feelings," she said.

"How do you know he loves you?" I asked

She showed me a gift packed in pink paper and said, "Every year on my birthday he gifts me the same thing in the same type of pack."

"By the way what's it?" I asked.

"It must be a musical dancing couple in glass," she was very confidently.

She opened it and really it was what she had said.

"This is the 5th year that he has given this to me," she said.

"How you know its Rahul who is gifting you every year like this as he is for the first time present on your birthday" I asked in confusion.

"It is true, because every year this gift was delivered by different kids," she said.

"But how do you know it is from his side" I asked again in confusion.

"Smell it bhaia... from these gifts a typical smell comes which belongs only to Rahul," she said bashfully.

I was impressed with her divine love and saluting her love. How can a girl remain so strong and confident regarding her love for so many years though there has been no progress?

"You want me to mediate?" I asked.

She didn't say anything and I got the answer.

# Rahul's Reality: A surprise of Life time

We had our dinner and turned to our hostel. At night I discussed everything with Robin and decided to do something for Shivani. Rahul had never talked about girls and been least interested in girls' affairs so asking him was a bit problematic. Though he was our friend we did not know him completely. Also, he was least talkative. Robin took this responsibility.

Next day Rahul was with Mohit discussing his assignment.

"Robin... Rahul is sitting there, I think this is the right time," I pointed at Rahul.

"Yes... I must talk to him now," he said and moved towards Rahul

"Robin… handle the issue carefully," I cautioned.

"Rahul, I want to talk to you" Robin said.

"What is the matter? You look tense." Rahul asked.

"Can I talk to you in private?" Robin asked.

"Yes... sure."

They went towards the basket ball ground.

"Rahul I am going to tell and ask you something," Robin said turning serious.

"Something very serious, very special," he added.

"Is everything alright?" Rahul asked.

"No...Nothing alright, but it may be alright for ever," he replied.

"How do you rate Shivani as a girl?" he asked.

"How and why I am supposed to rate her?" Rahul said

"Only you can rate her, our rating will not make any difference," Robin replied.

"I didn't get you," Rahul said in confusion.

"Ok...Let me be very clear. It's a very simple but delicate issue," Robin said.

"You are not a kid; don't you know Shivani loves you?" Robin said.

"She loves you since childhood but you never paid your attention to her love," he added.

"I have a sister but I love Shivani more than my own sister. If she is fine I am fine and if she suffers then I suffer," he added.

Rahul was listening to Robin silently with bowed head.

"Do you love her?" Robin asked.

At once Rahul looked at Robin but didn't reply. He again bowed his head.

"Do you love Shivani?" he again asked.

"Shut up now..." he shouted and turned in the other direction.

"No I will not shut up as you have already shut your mouth for years," Robin held his arm and pulled him.

"Is she ugly? Is she a bad girl? Is she a characterless?" Robin shouted

"Robin..." Rahul raised his hands in order to thrash Robin.

"I have got my answer, now you need not to reply." Robin said.

"But why don't you say it to Shivani? She is also dying for you every moment," he said.

"She is a good girl she will find a better guy than me," Rahul said.

"She doesn't want a better guy, she needs you in her life," Robin convinced him.

"I am not a suitable guy for her," Rahul said.

"Why you are saying this? No one can be better than you for her," Robin said.

"No further arguments ..." Rahul interrupted Robin.

"You will have to tell me the reason today," Robin said.

At once Rahul's face turned red and eyes became moist. He pushed Robin away saying, "I am not a right choice for her."

I was looking at all these from the other side. I sensed that there was something wrong. Robin narrated me everything. We both were worried now not only for Shivani but also for Rahul as there was something which was eating him up too.

Soon the year came to an end. It was our last exam. Anatomy exam had not gone very well for Robin. He was afraid of failure though he had really prepared hard. My exams went off well and I was expecting good marks.

I and Robin planned a small party at Mejbaan restaurant in Ber sarai.

"Call Rahul and inform him about the party," Robin said.

"Ya... I will call him on his number" and I dialed his number.

"His mobile is switched off," I said with disappointment

"Call one more time," Robin insisted.

"What do you think a second time it will switch on automatically?" I said and dialed

"Fuck... Switched off." I said.

"Where can he be?" Robin mumbled.

"I don't have any idea, may be he is somewhere near the canteen," I hazarded a guess.

"Let's go find him," Robin said and moved towards the canteen.

Suddenly Robin got a call from his parents and was engaged in talking. I moved towards the canteen. I saw a few friends of Rahul with whom he used to sit occasionally.

"Hey man, have you seen Rahul?" I asked.

"No buddy... he was here an hour ago," he informed

As I turned to go one of them said "Wait... I guess he is with Mohit."

"Where could they have gone?" I asked.

"I guess they will be in Mohit's room," he replied.

"Thanks buddy," I said and moved towards Chandrashekhar hostel.

I asked Mohit's room number from security. The hostel was calm as most of the students were partying after a series of exams.

"Room number 216" I murmured.

As I held the holder of gate it slipped inward and almost opened. To my shock and surprise I saw two guys intimately entwined as if they were one body. My heart beat became faster and my hands and feet started trembling. I could have never imagined Rahul in such a condition even in my wildest dream. They also looked at me and were just as shocked by my presence. I moved out and shut the door at once. After five minutes Rahul came out wearing his clothes. He was standing beside me silently with bowed head.

"Rahul... we have planned a party at Mejban at 8 o' clock today. I had come to inform you," I said.

"Ok... I will be there," he said in a choked voice.

I came back to my room, Robin was sleeping. As I got in to the room he woke up and said, "Did you find Rahul?"

"Yes... I informed him," I couldn't speak more.

I threw myself in bed. I still did not believe what I had seen. My head was aching. When I fell asleep I didn't know whether in my dream I had seen the whole thing. It was no less than a nightmare. My eyes opened as my heart beat became faster and I couldn't breadth well. Sometimes I regretted that I didn't know much about Rahul but it was even more regretting to know something like this about Rahul. Above all I was worried about my sister. How would she feel when she will come to know? Perhaps it will be the most shocking news for Shivani. Shivani father expired when she was only twelve years old. She had many problems of her house but still she was the liveliest girl I had ever seen. Above all I was worrying for the love which was the base of life of Shivani. Her love for Rahul was above all and it was to be shattered any time. I was confused, should I tell Robin or not?

Should I tell Shivani I was wondering? I was struggling with several such thoughts. I was not able to take any decision.

Would Rahul come to the party?

How would he face me and vice versa?

At last I was interrupted by Robin, "Hero we have to go, get dressed fast."

# Secret behind Rahul's reality

We reached Mejban before time. On the way Robin read my face and asked many times about my bad mood. I had no answer so I didn't say anything. We entered Mejban and to my surprise I saw Rahul waiting for us. We had a formal greeting. We ordered our meal. Robin was doing all pranks but Rahul and I were lost in a common world where we both were confused and sad and so remained silent.

"What happened to you guys?" Robin stroked our shoulders.

"Nothing….." I and Rahul spoke together.

"There is something wrong I can sense it, and you both say nothing? Right now it is the proof that there is something," he said.

Rahul was looking at me as if he was thanking me not disgracing him before Robin. This party was just like a funeral scene in which Shivani's love was getting its last act. We came out of Mejban. It was a pleasant night but someone has really said well "good mind good find" and our mind except Robin's were not fine. Perhaps I was worried about Robin because he was a very emotional guy if he came to know about Rahul God forbid?

"Let's have some beer or wine... What do you guys say?" Robin said.

"No Robin, let's get back to hostel," I suggested.

"What is there in the hostel idiot, its party time," he said.

"I have to watch a movie today at any cost," I lied.

"O shut up you fucker... What about you?" he asked Rahul.

"Ya... ya we can have it today," Rahul replied.

I was looking at Rahul with surprise. He too looked at me but it seemed he was determined.

"Then it's fixed, we are going to a beer bar," he said and turned towards his bike.

We too followed him as now nothing could be done in case of Robin. He didn't inform us, he ordered us. We went to a bar in South Ex.

"What will you have, sir?" the waiter asked.

"Anything which can set us free from hangover of exam and set our soul to ride the wind to a beautiful world" Robin said with a peculiar gesture.

"Russian vodka can do it for you sir," the waiter suggested.

"Then what are you waiting for? Bring it now," Robin said.

"Not more than two pegs Robin," I said.

"What happened to you? You are speaking like a fucker, and please don't fuck my mind," he said.

We had peg after peg and after a while I stopped counting as my brain was not able to do it.

"Sir, its closing time," a waiter came and said.

"What you say buddy, we just came here, want to have some more fun and you are saying its closing time," Robin stammered.

"Sir we every day close by 2 o' clock," the waiter informed.

"This is bad yaar, how we can have fun now?" Robin said

"Ok… Do one thing give us three bottle of beer and we will leave" Robin said.

"Sir now I can't help you as it is already closed," the waiter said.

"Where is the manager of this bar?" Robin shouted.

A man inside a black glass chamber asked the waiter to send Robin.

"I am just coming," Robin said and stood up.

"Let's go Robin… that man doesn't seem good," I suggested.

"Have patience, don't worry if he is not good what you think I am less than his father?" he said.

He went inside. We could see only Robin and that man talking. He was a thin man, with proper moustache and to my surprise he was having many gold chains around his neck and ring in every finger leaving thumb. Some serious conversation was going on between them and that bastard Robin was talking to him with his chest expended with fucking Rajput pride. At last that man wrote something on a piece of paper and gave it to Robin. Robin came back and handed over that paper to waiter and waiter went. To my surprise the waiter came back soon with three chilled beer bottles. We just paid for vodka these beer bottles were a gift of the manager to Robin. We collected the bottles and came out of the beer bar.

"What now Robin?" I asked.

"Let's go to PSR of JNU" he suggested.

JNU was a good hang out and Rahul's house was not far from

JNU North gate, so we agreed for PSR.

PSR was like semi forest with big rocks. In summers it uses to be the most popular hangout of students and outsiders. Love birds had all the privacy in forestry atmosphere with big rocks which cover them properly at nights. You can be as intimate as you have ever fantasized. We found a big rock and set there.

"Guys it's a great night," Robin said.

"Look the world is so beautiful if you have girl friends; you can have a real fun here if you have a GF". He said and stood on the rock.

A little misbalance and one can fall down and I am sure he will lose his life.

"Robin Don't stand on the rock, it's risky," I said.

"A Rajput isn't afraid of death," he said proudly.

"Shut up you rascal, sit or I will slap you hard," I said and stood up.

He sat down quietly.

"Guys I am going to tell you something," Rahul suddenly said.

"Oh ya... you will say something? Interesting... tell we are listening," Robin laughed

"It's something which I didn't tell anybody, not even my parents," he said with a sigh.

"First of all I want to say something which Raj didn't tell you Robin" he said and looked at me.

"What is going on? I don't get you people?" Robin said

"Today Raj saw me intimate with Mohit," Rahul said at once.

"Whaaat? You and Mohit? You mean…" Robin said but couldn't complete.

"Ya... I am a gay," Rahul said in one breadth.

"Oh no... My sister will die!"

I tried to console him but he at once jerked my hands away.

"See what this rascal is saying? He is a bloody gay" Robin sobbed.

"Raj… what will we say to Shivani?" he added.

"Robin I had already told you I am not of her type," Rahul said.

"Oh shut up... you can be a gay but you can't love the loveliest girl on the earth," Robin shouted.

"What you think it doesn't hurt me? My heart too beats for her but I am not suitable for her, she can have any better guy," Rahul said with grief stricken face.

"I could have cheated her as I know she loves me very much but I can't do that," he added.

"Since when you found out your gay?" I asked.

"Since last 2 years but first event was when I was just 13 years old" Rahul said.

"What? At an age of thirteen you were a gay? How it's possible?" I asked with surprise.

"What you think I was a gay since my childhood?" Rahul said.

"No... I was a normal guy but that event made me abnormal" he said.

"Which event? Will you make it clear?" asked Robin being irritated.

"It was the time when Madhu, my sister was in later months of her pregnancy. I with my mom went to look after her. She had a flat of two rooms. My mother used to sleep in one room with Madhu and I with my brother- in- law. As such my brother- in- law had never any love and affection for me but these were the days when I saw a change in his attitude. He used to kiss me sometimes. One night when I was asleep he unbuttoned my trouser and sexually abused me"

"Bastard... I will kill him," Robin shouted and hit on a rock.

"I too wanted to," Rahul said.

"Why you didn't take any action against him?" I asked.

The very next day before I could say it to any one he called me and said "I know you love your sister; you also know she is pregnant and she is always ill, so if you tell anybody about last night's event I will leave your sister then you can imagine how her life will be?"

"So better let's have a deal: you don't tell anybody and I will look after your sister until your mouth is shut," he forwarded his hand and unwillingly I too.

"This was the deal and in order to keep it a secret I lost my every thing," Rahul said.

"I always knew Shivani loved me but I always found myself not suitable for her, so I always avoided her," he explained.

"But I couldn't shake Shivani's love and many times I too found myself in love with her but you tell me is it right?" he said and broke down.

We all three cried.

"But why you are practicing it now?" I asked.

"It is just because I need it, how else I can solve my sexual urge?" he said.

"Mohit gave me some indication and we came closer and now we are practicing it" he explained.

"Can't you leave it?" Robin asked.

"For whom?" Rahul asked.

"For Shivani, for our friendship," Robin said.

"Will you and Shivani accept me?" Rahul asked.

"You were harassed; it was not your fault. It had to happen, but now if you promise to change we heartily welcome you," Robin said and stretched out his hands.

"Yes Rahul... we want you back and Shivani needs you the most" I said and I also stretched my hands. I and Robin hugged him and tears were dropping continuously. Now there was no pain, our hearts were full of love for each other. We drank all the beer and danced. This was the end of a chapter which brought us more close and made our friendship stronger.

# Love v/s friendship

We returned to Safdurjung Enclave at 4 o' clock in the morning. How we came back we only know. Many times we were about to fall down from our bikes but somehow we managed to return. We were drunk up to our neck. Rahul came to our hostel along us. We fell on our bed; I shared my bed with Rahul. Soon the room was flooded with snoring of my friends and I was restless. I was not able to sleep. I was worried that if I fell sleep with this restlessness I would not awake up ever. I left the bed and lit a cigarette and then lit another. I was pacing the room and sometimes looked out of the window. I opened the door and slinked out. I was clueless where I was going? I kept moving, better to say stumbling as it was difficult to walk straight due to intoxication. Suddenly my steps became frail. I stood for sometimes and looked around. It was very difficult to identify the place.

There I saw a statue, I moved towards it. It seemed as it was a statue of a woman. I looked at her continuously and suddenly my heart filled with pain.

I started talking to the statue.

"So you are a woman?"

"Very good… you know my name? I am Rajvardhan"

"Leave it... what you have to take with my name?"

"Can we have friendship?"

"Leave it... I don't need any friendship from any girl"

"Do you know why?"

"How will you know? I tell you. I tried for a girl's friendship but you know unfortunately she was the dream girl of my best friend."

"How sad... isn't it? I committed an unintentional crime, I can never forgive myself"

"I am in friendship with my friend still today, but somewhere he is still hurt from me"

"I avoid the girl and I avoid my love for her but do you know I am suffering with each breath."

"I broke my friend's heart, I am suffering for girl but that girl doesn't know anything"

"You can evaluate how lucky I am?"

"Loving a girl is wrong? No... But loving your friend's girl is not just wrong, it is sin."

"Do you know her name?"

"Again how you will know? I tell you"

"Hey stop... I will not tell you, winds are mischievous as they may slander to my friend and again he will be hurt"

"Better I write it as stupid winds are illiterate they can't read, ha ha ha.."

During all these monologue my eyes dropped uncounted tears.

"How to write? I don't have a pen," I mumbled.

I saw a blade lying on the ground, I picked it from there anyhow and cut my index finger badly and with my blood I wrote CH on the statue and suddenly I fell down. After that I don't know what happened?

When I opened my eyes I found myself in my room. I had a bad hangover and my head was aching a lot. I saw Rahul and Robin discussing something very seriously at other end of the room. I tried to collect my senses and moved toward them staggering. When they saw me they stopped the discussion and Rahul came forward to support me.

"What's going on guys?" I asked.

"Is there anything serious? You people look tensed," I added.

"First of all you tell us where you went at 4 o' clock?" Rahul asked.

"I left somewhere? I don't remember?" I said.

"You don't remember anything? You left the room, reached Indira hostel" Rahul said.

At once Robin left the room. We both looked at Robin.

"Rahul what I did there?" I asked.

"I don't know what you did there but at around 7 o' clock we got a call from the hostel reception that you are lying near a statue," he explained.

"Then?" I asked in curiosity and fear.

"Then what? We at once left for Indira hostel and carried you here," he said.

"What you did there you will tell us and why you went there?" Rahul asked.

"I really don't remember anything" I said scratching my head.

Suddenly I became fearful  thinking that I must have again hurt Robin. I ran out, Rahul followed me. I saw Robin sitting on the fence of the hostel. I went near him.

"Robin... I don't remember anything," I said.

"What dragged me there I don't know? But any way I again hurt you," I said with bowed head.

"I don't know why it happens with me only? Why I always hurt you? I can't be your friend"

Robin turned his head other side.

"I know it will be tough for you to forgive me but try to forgive me, I will no longer stay here to hurt you," I added.

Rahul was looking this all from a little distance. I returned to room and started packing my luggage. I was tearful and was cursing myself for coming to DIMS. I suffered all the time and made my friend suffer too. I was all set to quit medical college and I also had no answer for my father's question regarding it. Suddenly Robin and Rahul entered the room.

"Why you are packing your suitcase?" Rahul asked.

"I am quitting college," I replied.

"Permanently?" he asked.

"Yes... I have no reason to continue," I replied in choked voice.

"You want to go, you may go but before that you will have to pay every moment for my sufferings," Robin said with a tough look.

"Ya... Anything for you..." I turned at him and said.

"Come with me then," he held my hand dragged me outside.

He made me sit on his bike and drove it towards Indira hostel in full speed. It seemed he was all set to commit suicide with me at Indira hostel. He pulled me to the statue.

"Look what you have done?" he said by pointing at the statue.

CH was written at statue with blood.

"What is this?" he asked.

Suddenly everything started striking my brain. It started paining a lot and I held my head with my hands and pressed it. I recalled everything which I did yesterday.

"Robin I was drunk and was not aware what I was doing?" I said.

"You cut your finger badly, have you seen that?" he said.

I looked at once at my finger and screamed, "Oh crap, fuck"

I had not noticed my finger since when I left the bed so it was not paining but now according to conditional reflex it started paining a lot.

"It was good that you lost your senses and didn't complete Charulata's name" he gnashed.

"Do you know what could have happened?" he added.

I was listening silently.

"Charu is all yours Robin I am leaving college today, forgive me" I said.

"No chance... first pay my debt and then if you want to leave you may," he said again gnashing his teeth.

"What I can do for you?" I said with bowed head.

"Propose Charu, don't leave her instead love her and forgive me as just because of me you suffered a lot," Robin said and became tearful.

"You sacrificed your love in order to keep your friendship alive, you suffered a lot but never complained, I am proud of you darling," he said and hugged me.

We cried for long hugging each other. We heard voices of girls and got separated. We turned at them, to our surprise near about fifty girls were surrounding us and were murmuring.

"Look … gays!" one of them said.

"O madam..." I said and moved towards her.

Robin held my hand and stopped me approaching her. Rahul too reached there.

"Look at this gay, he is not even wearing his trousers," one of the girl said pointed at me.

I looked my self from up to down and screamed, really I had worn only a short and that too was like an underwear. I attempted unsuccessfully to pull it down and make it longer.

"Leave it Raj, if you will try hard to adjust it your bums will show," Robin said and all started laughing.

"Why don't you people practice it in your rooms?" a girl shouted.

"Sorry ma'am it will be in rooms only from next time," Robin replied gesticulating like a eunuch.

"Shut up you fucker," I shouted at Robin. "We are not gay."

"If you want me to be happy do what I said, we are friends and nothing can shake our friendship," he said and both Robin and Rahul hugged me.

Again girls started hooting at us. Robin held Rahul's hand and moved towards his bike. They rode on the bike and moved towards Kabir hostel.

"Where you are going?" I shouted.

"To our hostel, you may also come but by using your feet" Robin shouted.

"Stop... Stop... behencho," I shouted at them.

"Our hostel is far away and how will I go there like this?" I murmured

I hit the statue.

"O my God... Fuck" my finger started paining with that hit.

I looked around and still the crowd was surrounding me.

"I am not a gay… get lost all of you," I shouted.

Perhaps this time shouting was more intensive as the crowd started dispersing.

"I am not a gay," I shouted several times and moved towards Kabir hostel.

On the way many people looked at me sarcastically and laughed and I abused Robin five times, but I was relaxed as my friend has not only forgiven me but also set me free to bloom my love bud.

# Charu: Beauty with Brain

We went home on vacation. We again came back to start second year. After one month again life screwed like hell. We worked like donkeys in order to maintain our average and reputation. Result too was to be published soon so our days used to be restless and nights without proper sleep. Perhaps these are the days during which medicos suffer from diseases like insomnia, digestive tract problems like gastritis, ulcers and many more. Any way the result was published. There was a crowd at the administrative building. We too rushed to it. I was praying to my Gods. Rahul was also a bit nervous but Robin was cool.

"You seem so cool at this moment?" I asked.

"What should I do then? Should I be tensed as you people are?" Robin said driving bike.

I didn't say anything. Making way through the crowd was not easy but I incited Robin, I challenged his Rajput ego and it worked. He made way and we started running our eyes on the merit list.

"Where is my name? Fuck…" I shouted.

"It has written alphabetically so you must find it under R for all three of us," Robin suggested.

At last I saw it.

"Rajvardhan Sahay.. 73%, Rahul Tyagi.. 84% and Robin 62%" I murmered.

"We have all passed," I shouted.

Rahul was a bit sad with his marks. However he was third overall.

"Are not you happy Rahul?" I asked.

"I am happy but I was expecting better marks," he replied in a low tone.

"Rahul always be happy for which you get. Never complain as after everything God checks us and if we complain we are declared fail in his exam and if we show faith in his judgments then he rewards us next time. So have faith and don't be sad and see what happens to you in the next exam" Robin said and caressed his head.

Robin continued impressing me.

Soon college published the results of third year. We three were in the canteen for lunch. Few seniors were discussing the result.

"Do you know how much Charulata has scored?" I asked inquisitively.

"Charulata Chaudhry or Charulata Saxena?" he asked.

"Are there two Charulatas?" I murmured.

"One Charulata stays in Indira Hostel and the other in Sarojini Hostel," he informed.

"Charulata who lives in Indira hostel" I said.

"She topped the exams," he said.

Our food came out of our mouths. What a joke of circumstance? Already I had many problems regarding my love with her now a new one came to light. She was a scholar to boot. I looked at both of my friend one by one. They were clueless. I didn't eat only drank water in order to digest the new fact.

"What to do now?" I asked.

There was a complete silence and then Robin said "You must wish her at least."

I looked angrily at him.

"Ya... she deserves it, go and wish her with beautiful roses," Robin suggested.

Rahul too supported Robin.

"Let's go out side to pick some beautiful roses for the successful lady," Robin said and stood up.

We went South Ex and bought flowers for her and came back. Robin asked a senior about Charu and he informed she was at Mamu's canteen. We reached there and on the way my heart beats were so fast that I perspired a lot and it seemed I would die of heart attack.

"Be cool yaar... you are not going for a war and stop overstraining your heart as I can hear your heart beats," Robin said.

"Is proposing a girl less than a war?" I said.

"Are you proposing her today? WOW!" he sarcastically said.

"NO...NO... I will wish her only and that too if I can collect that much courage," I cleared.

Soon we reached there and seeing the crowd I just gave up the idea of wishing her.

"Robin... I can't wish her at this moment and place," I said in fear.

"Why? What happened?" he asked.

"Can't you see the crowd? I don't know how she will take this or how she will behave?" I said.

"You are here just to wish her and I don't know a single reason why she will take it otherwise," he said pushing me towards the crowd.

"Yaar I am afraid...Let's go home and rethink on it" I said and turned back.

"She will be greeted today and right now either you yourself go and greet her or I will greet her on your behalf" he said and grabbed the flowers.

Again this erratic Rajput was a problem as he perhaps committed himself for this task.

With a heavy heart I entered the crowd again. The way was made by Robin. Robin left behind and I crossed few people there but my courage failed and I couldn't cross few more people in order to approach Charu. I kept standing there for long and kept enjoying all the gestures of her. She was very happy and her hands were full of flowers. I looked at my flowers and found them unlucky. I kept standing few more minutes and then turned back to come out.

"Raj..." someone shouted.

"I stopped in my steps and strained my ears to find out if I had actually heard my name.

"Raj vardhan" again the same voice.

I turned back and found Charu coming towards me.

I quickly hid the flowers.

"What a pleasant surprise to see you here," she said.

"I was going somewhere and saw this crowd and came in to see what's going on," I tried to explain.

"You are not a good liar but I tell you we are here partying because as I have topped the exam," she said.

Her last sentenced further discouraged me.

"Oh that's great in deed. Congratulations" I greeted her.

"Please have something, you don't know how happy I am to see you after such a long time," she said.

"Perhaps you have forgotten me?" she added looking sad.

I thought in my mind "It is not easy to forget you alas you knew how much I love you."

"Oye... Where are you lost?" she said

"No nothing... I have to leave now," I said.

"You really want to leave?" she asked.

I again thought in my mind "I wish I could never leave you, this time just stop itself here but the crowd is the villain."

"Are you alright? Where you lose yourself?" she asked.

"Where else except you?" I mumbled.

"What?" she asked with a smile.

"Ya, I want to leave as Robin is waiting outside," I said and turned hiding the flowers.

"Didn't you forget something?" she asked.

"What? Did I?" I pretended.

"Perhaps those flowers are for me," she said smiling.

I nearly fainted.

"If those are not for me than you may leave," she said.

"Actually these flowers are for you only, please accept it." I said handing over them to her.

"So sweet of you..." she said putting all flowers on the table by the side and holding my flowers only.

"I know you are not comfortable here. Let us have a private party," she suggested.

"I will be in the library only after 4 o' clock, do inform me when you will have time" she said smelling the flowers.

"Ya... sure definitely," I replied.

I came out as if I had conquered the world.

"What happened Fattu?" Robin asked.

"I handed over the flowers to her and she asked me for a private party," I said smiling.

"Oh that's good... so when you are going?" he asked.

"We have not decided yet yaar... lets get back to hostel," I said.

"Any way she is going to perish on you any damn day," Robin said with confidence.

# A Perfect Unofficial Date

Every year in month of October there used to be a sports wave in which every house used to be in competition to win all the trophies. Not only the sports but there used to be Inter college fashion show and Mr. Medico and Miss Medico used to be selected. It was a high time for me to practice cricket as I was one of the best players of my house. Girl's hostels were evenly distributed among houses like Sarojini hostel became Kabir house's representative in Woman sports and Indira hostel was the representative of Nanak house. We had ten houses and all came in battle ground for proving themselves the best house of the year. This was the time when nobody was interested in classes and every house in its own way was making strategies and manipulating the resources to show other house inferior in each field. In other words it was a high time for politics.

One day I was practicing on ground with my team, when I saw a lady moving her hand from the library's window. It was Charu and seemed as if she was calling me.

"Guys... you carry on I am just coming," I said and moved.

I reached at library's main gate and I saw Charu reading a medical journal at little distance at window. I entered and moved to her. She didn't notice me or she pretended not to see me.

"Hello... ma'am," I greeted.

"Oh... I am sorry I didn't see you... hello," she replied.

"You called me?" I asked.

"Me? No..." she said being surprised.

"I was playing cricket and it seemed you were beckoning me with your hands," I said.

"No, my friend Rajesh was on the ground and I was greeting him," she said.

"Ok... I am sorry I mistook it," I said being ashamed.

Her last line was striking my brain and I became disappointed after hearing the name Rajesh.

"Bye... Have a nice time" I said and turned back to go out.

"Stop... You are really a duffer, can't you judge I was telling a lie actually I called you" she said with a smile.

"Ma'am why you will tell a lie actually I mistook" I said.

"Stop calling me ma'am... Am I that older than you?" she asked

"Then what I should call you?" I asked.

"Call me by my name, don't you like my name?" she asked.

"No, I mean yes, your name is very beautiful but how I can call you by your name?" I said in nervousness.

"In medicine every body belongs to the same community and I am only a year senior to you, you can call me by my name, I don't have any problem," she explained.

"How can you play all the time?" she asked.

"Sports competition between the Houses is coming nearer, so I have to practice," I said.

"Your flowers were very beautiful and lovely," she said.

"If it gave you a single smile I think those were really nice," I replied.

"Why are your eyes red?" she asked.

"Are they? I don't know. May be because I didn't sleep well last night," I replied.

"Why? What happened at night?" she asked.

"Nothing much but I just kept changing sides on bed," I replied a bit nervously.

"Who tormented you all night? Is it a girl?" she asked and laughed.

After her last sentence I realized what dialogues were going on between us as I did not say all intentionally. Suddenly I blushed.

"What are you doing today evening?" she asked. "Nothing as such," I replied.

"Can we go out as I have promised you a party," she asked.

"Sure ma'am..." I nodded my head.

"Again ma'am?" she reprimanded.

"If you can call me by my name then only we will go out," she said becoming angry.

"I will wait for you at 5 o' clock at Indira hostel's gate" she said.

She said and left. I stared at her till she became out of sight.

"Definitely you are Charu and for me only," I murmured.

I came back on the ground and in excitement hit many boundaries. During lunch time I told everything to Rahul and Robin. They were happy with the recent progress.

"You must go on a date but maintain your dignity," Robin said.

"What do you mean by maintaining dignity?" Rahul asked.

"Maintaining dignity means don't give her much privilege as I guess she is very interested in you so do not propose to her at once," Robin said.

"Then when I should propose her?" I asked.

"I don't think you will need to propose to her as she may propose you, let her propose you," Robin said.

"What nonsense Robin? Can a girl propose to a guy even though she is madly in love with him?" Rahul said being irritated.

"Why not? If she doesn't propose then you propose to her, but till that time make her writhe as she has made you," Robin said.

"Let her taste how it feels to be in love?" Robin added.

Rahul and I looked unsatisfied with Robin's argument but we both agreed as Robin had a vision. His tips had helped many guys; he was Love Guru of DIMS in other words.

Time was like Draupadi's cheer as it was not ready to pass, and even five minutes seemed like five years. I tried many things to pass the time but all the time my eyes to my watch. Heart beats got fast and slow as it happens in arrhythmia. In excitement I couldn't even eat as if I had anorexia, and although my eyes were red and sleepy but I could not sleep, as if I had insomnia. I was a body suffering from love attack and these were the symptoms of the disease but unfortunately medical science has not developed any medicine and prophylaxis for this ailment! I wish medical science should take it seriously and think on my proposal "If you are in love…you need medicine."

I thought to get ready and pass the time but it took only twenty minutes to get dressed even after a great deal of wastage of time. At 5 o' clock I reached Indira hostel on my bike. Charu was waiting outside.

"You are on time, I like it," she said as she came forward.

"Where are we going?" I asked.

"Anywhere you like but let's go some place where we can spend a few hours," she said.

"Few hours…? Great…" I thought in my mind and smiled.

"Do you know any such place?" she asked.

"I am not sure but I guess Priya will be the best," I said.

"Yes, you are right, let's go there," she agreed and sat on my bike.

Life could be so meaningful to me I had never imagined. She gradually put her hands on my shoulders. It was hard to drive the bike as every touch of hers was intoxicating.

"O God if it is a dream never let me wake up," I thought in my mind.

Sometimes her hair used to fly and kiss my cheek and several times I too kissed them silently.

We reached Priya's and I parked the bike. We took one round of Priya's. She looked at some girly items like ear rings, nose rings and hair bands. She liked one ear ring but didn't buy it. I was following her.

"Let's park ourselves in Barista," she said. I nodded in agreement.

Barista was jam-packed; however, we got a place as a couple left.

"What you would like to have?" she asked.

"Only a cup of coffee," I replied.

"Only coffee? Have something else with it," she said.

"Thanks but I am not hungry," I replied.

She stood up and went to the counter and ordered.

"So how is your preparation for the tournament going on?" she asked.

"I guess well…" I replied.

"In how many events are you participating?"

"Mainly in cricket but I have been nominated for volleyball and badminton too," I replied.

"Nice yaar… so you must be the gem of your house," she said with smile.

"I don't know about that but I want to win for my house," I replied.

"Aren't you participating?" I asked.

"I didn't want to but my house has nominated me for painting and beauty contest," she replied.

"Oh… that means you are the contestant for Miss Medico?" I asked.

"Ya… for the time being, as I have never done it before and I don't want it now even but house committee is not ready to listen," she said helplessly.

"What's wrong in it? You should participate as you have all the chances of winning," I said with confidence.

"Do you really think so?" she asked smiling

"Yes, I am sure," I replied.

"Your house has selected Nidhi Garg, a final year student. I think she has all chances of winning," she said.

"I wish the deserving candidate wins," I said.

She smiled.

The waiter interrupted us with our orders. She had ordered a cake along with her cold coffee. I started sipping my coffee and she hers.

"Hey taste this cake," she said abruptly forwarding me her spoon.

"No... I am ok with this coffee," I hesitated.

"Taste it right now, it is so tasty," she insisted.

"I don't have a spoon," I gave a lame excuse.

"Hmm... take mine," she said. "Or do you mind taking somebody's offal?" she asked.

"It's not that ...but how will you use it after me?" I asked.

"It doesn't bother me, I too don't use offal but I have changed many rules of my life," she said.

I held her spoon and took a spoonful cake and gulped it down. It was really nice.

"Thanks... It is really awesome but I can't eat anymore," I pleaded.

She didn't say anything and again engaged with her cake.

"Excuse me... I am just coming," I said.

"Where you are going?" she asked.

"Just coming," I said.

"Don't worry, you don't have to pay the bill so don't run away," she said laughing.

After five minutes I came back.

"I thought you had run away," she grinned and said.

Having seen her pearly teeth I could not resist myself from smiling.

"Its 7 o' clock, let's go now," she said.

"Ya sure," I stood up.

She collected her bag and just as she turned, her bag brushed against the glass and it fell down with a crash and broke. Every one including me turned towards Charu.

"Oh I am so sorry," she said in an embarrassed manner.

Her face was so innocent that even it was her fault anybody would have forgiven her for any damn crime and this was a small thing.

"Don't worry, every thing is fine," I said and moved towards the counter.

I offered to pay for the glass but the boy at the counter refused. When I insisted he said, "It was an accident. Don't worry, come again sir."

We came out of Barista. All the way she didn't say anything.

"Here, we have reached your hostel," I said.

She got down of the bike and stood quietly.

"Thank you for this great evening," I said.

"I am sorry, it was not intentional what happened in Barista," she said looking disappointed.

"Oh my God you are still thinking about that?" I said.

"I thought you too had a great evening but I am wrong," I said pretending to be sad.

"I too had a great evening till the glass broke," she said.

"I have something for you" I said and forwarded my closed fist.

"What's it?" she asked.

"Give me your hand but close your eyes first," I instructed.

She did like that and I kept it on her palm.

She opened her eyes and squealed with delight, "Oh my God... how did you guess I had liked this ear ring?"

"Just like that Charu," I said.

"What? What you said right now?" she asked.

"Just like that" I replied.

"No, after that?" she asked.

I hesitated a bit but said "Charu."

"I am so happy to hear my name from your mouth," she smiled.

"Thank you for every thing Raj. It was really one of the pleasantest evenings I have ever had," she said thanking me.

"I must leave now," she said in a low tone.

"Ya... sure," I said.

"See you, bye," she said and turned to go.

"Hey... if you don't mind can I have your mobile number?" I asked.

"Ya sure but you are asking me for it after one year we met first time," she said. "Anyway, write…" she dictated the number and I typed it in my contact address.

"Give me a miss call right now, she said.

I called her.

"Thank you," I said.

"My pleasure, but please don't be formal with me as I like it when you are natural," she smiled and said.

I came back hostel and described every thing to Robin.

"That's like a brave man, this is called dance at a chance," Robin said stroking my back.

# Annual Inter-house Competitions

$T$ he fever of our college sports competition was at its peak. Everyday we had a tournament or the other which turned into a pitched battle later. Our house was doing very well. Robin and I dominated in cricket and won the trophy for our house. I also won in badminton winning one more prize for my house.

Now it was the turn for the painting competition. Paintings from all houses were displayed in the exhibition hall. I was interested in Charu's paintings only. She was standing next to her paintings.

"Hey... how is your painting doing?" I asked.

"I don't know, it will be decided by the jury," she said.

"I hope you win. I don't know much about paintings but yours looks excellent," I said.

"I like your attitude, you are honest about your opinions," she said.

"But your house can win too as their entries are excellent," she said.

It was now time for the announcement of results. All of us gathered anxiously at the hall where the chief guest was to announce and give away the prizes.

"We got some really excellent paintings from our talented students from each house this time and our esteemed chief guest will soon announce the names of the winners," the principal said.

At once Charu held my hand holding her painting brush in the other hand. I looked down at my hand; it was looking very good with that delicate, soft and fair hand around it. I didn't look at Charu just in case she would sense and leave my hand.

The Chief Guest came on the dais holding the winner's name which was written on a colorful envelop. Charu's grip became more and more intense with every passing moment. Her nails were digging into my skin, it was painful but pleasurable too.

I looked at Charu's other hand; the brush was now kissing her cheeks and partially painted it green.

"And the winner is… Charulata Chaudhry, 3rd year Nanak House," chief guest announced.

"She was motionless for a moment and then suddenly her grip slackened and my breath came down. She looked at me. In order to make her realize the condition I jumped up and down several times saying "Charu you are the winner! You are the winner! Congrats!"

My house mates were staring me including Robin and Rahul. At once I came back to normal.

"Second prize goes to Nandini Shaha, Kabir house."

"Third Prize goes to Rajni Pathak, Nanak house."

The Principal again took the mike and requested this trio to come up to the stage one by one to take their prizes.

"Go... You are first," I nudged her.

She moved towards the dais and at once I held her hand, "Wait, don't go like this," I said and wiped the green paint off her cheeks...

She held her trophy, looked at her house and then looked at me for a few seconds as if her eyes were trying to say something to me.

She came back to me holding her trophy.

"I never imagined I would win this trophy," she said. "Even now I can't believe it," she added.

"But it's true, it is your own trophy in your own hand," I said and touched the trophy.

"Oh my God what happened to your hand?" she screamed.

I looked at my hand. It had turned blue black at a few places.

"It is nothing" I said and trying to hide it.

"Show me," she said and pulled my hand towards her.

"How did you get it?" she asked.

"You were in stress and in order to ease yourself you dug your nails in it," I said.

"Why didn't you tell me you idiot?" she scolded me.

"Let's go out and apply some ointment on it," she said and pushed me.

We went to her hostel. I waited for her in the visitor's room. She brought the ointment and applied it on my hands gently massaging it. I was looking down but I could feel her. Perhaps for such intimacy I wouldn't mind bearing some more such pains.

A week later Mr. and Miss Medico were to be announced after a few ramp shows. One day I and Robin were coming from South Ex and were standing at Banarasi Paan Bhandar for some paan and cigarettes.

"Hey Raj look over there," Robin suddenly said.

"Where?" I asked.

"Charu is there at the bus stop," he said pointing at the opposite direction.

"Yes, may be she going somewhere," I said.

"Idiot, look she is with a big bag," he said.

"Oh yes, where could she be going?" I asked.

"Go and ask her. May be she needs some help?" he said.

I ran towards Charu. Till that time her bus had arrived and she had got in.

"Charu... Charu... where are you going?" I asked.

"Raj... you?" she was surprised to see me.

"Ya me... but where are you going?" I asked again.

"I am going home," she replied.

"Home? Where? You are a Delhite ?" I said

"No, I am from Kolkata and I am going there," she said putting out her head out of the window.

"When are you coming back?" I asked in disappointment.

Robin sensed something was wrong, He ran towards the bus and tried to convince the driver to make the bus halt for a few minutes but the driver refused. So he stood in front of the bus, the driver startedhonking.

"I will be back within a week" she said.

"But you were contesting for Miss Medico. How can you leave, it is just after two days" I said with a disappointed face.

"I withdrew myself from the contest," she informed.

Meanwhile people came and tried to pull Robin away from the bus's way. A minor scuffle ensued and in the process Robin thrashed a few of them and himself got thrashed too. I ran towards Robin for his rescue and the bus driver drove away the bus seeing his way cleared. Police too arrived and warned us.

Charu left many questions unanswered behind. We came back to the hostel but my peace of mind had gone.

Miss Medico competition was boring for me without Charu. Kabir house won the title of Miss Medico with a wide margin. Our Kabir house was declared house of the year as it won six titles out of a total of ten. Our house had organized a party but I was in no mood to go. I called Charu's number constantly but her phone was switched off.

"She should have given me her house landline's number at least" I murmured.

# Love finds it's way: A New Beginning

"Raj let's go shopping," Robin suddenly said.

"No yaar... I don't feel to go," I replied.

"You need a change man, how long will you be mopping for her? She is alright and will come soon," he consoled.

"Robin... please, don't force me, ask Rahul," I said.

"Rahul is also coming and so is Shivani," he informed.

Robin left for Lajpat Nagar along with Rahul and Shivani.

It was the tenth day since I saw Charu. She said, she will be back in a week. What could have gone wrong? May be her parents had fixed her marriage? Several such questions started tormenting me.

Lajpat Nagar market is very big.

"Shivani... I have to meet a friend who lives close by," Robin said.

"So? What do you want to say?" Rahul glared at him.

"So... you people carry on I will join you as soon as possible," Robin said.

"You are not going anywhere," Rahul said angrily.

"Its urgent yaar I promise I will come back soon," Robin said and turned to go.

"You rascal, listen to me bastard" Rahul shouted at Robin but he went away laughing.

"If you have any problem staying with me, you can go with Robin bhaia, I can do shopping on my own," Shivani said.

"No...Shivani, it is not like that. I guess you will not be comfortable with me," Rahul said.

"It is always you who feels uncomfortable. For me you are the most comfortable person," she said complaining.

They started exploring the market. They looked at a few things but didn't buy and moved on.

"I am hungry," Shivani said.

"Ok...Let's go to a near by restaurant," Rahul said.

"No... I want to have momos," Shivani said.

"Momos? It is not at all a healthy food, it's junk," Rahul said.

"You doctors are really too much... food is food and sometimes we can have any food," she said and moved towards a thela selling momos.

Rahul silently followed her.

"Bhaia one plate momos please and this well dressed gentleman will pay you," she said and laughed.

Rahul paid money. There was a bench by the side of the thela, Shivani sat down on it and started to eat the momos dipping it in the special chilly sauce.

"Hey come and taste it, its really tasty," she said.

Rahul came and sat next to her and picked up a momo and started eating it slowly.

"Finish it fast... it will not kill you," Shivani said smilingly.

Rahul finished it and picked up another. He had perhaps tasted momos in his childhood but never touched it in the recent past.

They moved on again to explore the market. Shivani stood near a bangle shop and looked at some bangles. She liked a set and asked the shopkeeper "How much for this set?"

"250 rupees," he replied.

"My God! It is too costly, these people have set the market on fire" she complained.

She looked at another set and asked the price.

"175 rupees for this," the shopkeeper said.

"Won't you give any discount?" she asked.

"No madam, these are really very good items and that's why they are costly but you can give me ten rupees less," he said.

"150 is too much for this set," she argued.

"I will go at a loss then madam, if we will not earn at least ten rupees what's the use of sitting whole day like this," shopkeeper said.

"Bhaia I really liked it but obviously you don't want to sell it," Shivani said and turned to go.

"Madam I can give you but not less than 160 bucks, please understand my problem too," he said.

"Shivani if you really like it, please buy it," Rahul said.

"Ok bhaia... wrap it but be sure there should not be any cracked piece or I will return it to you," she warned.

"I am a bit surprised today," Shivani later said.

"Why?" Rahul asked.

"You are today very different from what you used to be earlier," Shivani said.

Rahul didn't reply and kept walking.

"Believe me, it is not less than a miracle," she said looking at Rahul.

Just then Rahul's mobile rang. It was Robin.

"Where are you people?"

"We are at Triveni Sari House," he replied.

"How was your time?" Robin asked.

"You come to me than I will say you behencho!" Rahul said angrily

"I am coming in five minutes but I also have something to say to you," he said and hung up.

"So Shivani you have done some shopping? What's this in this packet?" Robin asked.

"Bangles... did you find your friend?" she asked.

"That's what I want to tell you people that I couldn't meet my friend as a divine beauty crossed my path and I followed her all the time, suddenly she eloped and I came to you," Robin narrated the story but both Rahul and Shivani were looking somewhere.

"Bhaia I am just coming, I forgot to buy something," Shivani said and left.

"Robin... I too forgot to buy something, I am coming in five minutes," he said and left.

"What you did all these two hours behencho?" Robin shouted at Rahul.

"No one is cared about me," he grumbled.

In fifteen minutes they came back with something in their hand.

"Robin bhaia…. You were saying something," Shivani said.

"Ya Robin tell now," Rahul said

"Shut up you rascal" Robin shouted and started to walk away.

"Robin bhaia don't get angry, tell me at least," Shivani insisted.

"No... You also don't care for me" Robin complained.

"Shivani... Robin is not willing to say so we shouldn't force him" Rahul said and laughed.

"I will kill you... I will tell to Shivani only" Robin said angrily.

"Shivani actually I saw a girl in jeans and green top and she was so beautiful that I can't explain you" Robin started explaining.

"Bhaia... look at that girl. Isn't she that girl?" Shivani said pointing towards a girl.

Robin looked at her and shouted "Ya she is 100% the same girl!"

"Then why are you waiting? At least try to know who she is?" Shivani said.

"Don't go idiot, I am sure you will be beaten," Rahul pranked.

"I am a Rajput, I am not afraid of anything," he said and moved towards the girl.

Rahul and Shivani followed him. As Robin was about to get close to her she got into a car and drove away.

"Shit... bull shit!" Robin ranted.

"What happened Mr. Rajput?" Rahul said.

"No problem bhaia... if she would be your valentine and your feeling is strong and true for her you will meet her again" Shivani said and tried to console Robin.

They came back to the hostel and Shivani narrated me whole story. Robin was silent.

"So Rajput bhai, what next?" I asked Robin.

"Am I that stupid? I memorized her car number plate," Robin said.

"DL003 4229" he mumbled.

"I agree with Shivani, if my feeling for her is true and strong, she will come to me somewhere somehow" he said with confidence.

"Bhaia I should leave now as mom will be worrying," Shivani said.

"I should leave too," Rahul said.

"Ok... drop Shivani at her home," Robin said.

They moved out and I started discussing Charu and the unknown girl who was now Robin's latest crush.

Outside love was all set to make its presence felt. Rahul dropped Shivani home.

"Ok then... Good night," Rahul said.

"Rahul I have something for you," Shivani said and pushed a packet in his hands.

"Shivani actually I too have something for you," he said and forwarded a poly bag to her. They both accepted each others gift and thanked each other with their eyes. They both opened their gift and became so happy that tears started dropping.

It was a shirt which Rahul was looking at in the market and it was those bangles which Shivani had liked first time but didn't buy. Coming back home Rahul wore the shirt and Shivani the bangles and both looked at themselves in the mirror for half an hour, both imagining each other by their side — Rahul in that shirt and Shivani wearing those bangles. It was a dream which both always had in their eyes but time had robbed it from Rahul. Today a dream once again came and sat in Rahul's eyes in which he could see himself with Shivani.

# Love finds its way: Through hugs

One day when I was in the library, my mobile rang. It was Charu's call.

"Hello..." I spoke in a low tone.

"Raj... where are you?" she asked.

"I am in the library," I said.

"Oh that's good as I am near its gate, come out, are you studying?" she asked.

"No... I was here to issue a book," I said.

"Ok then come out" she said.

I came out and when I saw Charu my heart nearly came to my mouth out.

"Are not you happy to see me?" she asked.

"I am happy to see you but I am not happy the way you left me alone with many bad thoughts after your departure," I said.

"It was an emergency, I had to be at home without any delay," she said.

"If you don't mind can I know the emergency?" I asked.

"Yes sure... but not here, let's go somewhere else," she said.

We came to Subhas's canteen in our college and ordered tea.

I was all silent and Charu was looking at me.

"I guess I have hurt you a lot," she said.

"Definitely Charu, you could at least send me an SMS," I said being irritated.

She became silent and then I realized, she was not my girl friend and I shouldn't demand an explanation from her.

"I am sorry... I shouldn't ask you like this. I was just restless all these days so I reacted like this" I said apologizing.

"No...Its ok, I could have reacted in the same way too if someone close had done what I did," she said.

"My mom is a heart patient since ten years and she had a heart attack a few days before I left," she said and burst into tears.

I came close to her. "I am really sorry Charu," I said caressing her hair.

"It was very difficult to keep myself integrated when I heard this news, at that moment could I send you an SMS?" she said amidst tears.

"No... You did what a normal human being could have done" I said and tried to console her.

She stood up and stood in the canteen's corridor. I followed her. She was crying holding a pillar.

"Please don't cry, my heart will stop working, I can't see you like this" I said and caressing her head.

"My mom is alright but she will not live longer Raj," she said, turned to me and hugged me tightly.

"Charu she will be alright, how she can leave a daughter like you all alone" I said and consoled her.

"Every body leaves me alone, my father expired when I was just ten years old, now my mother is planning to leave me" she stammered with grief.

"Some day you will leave me too," she said.

"I will never leave you Charu, it's impossible," I assured her hugging her tightly.

At once her grip slacked, she separated herself from me.

"I am sorry, I am alright" she said and came back to the canteen.

Our teas were on the table. We were having our tea. I looked at Charu in between several times but she had her tea with bowed head.

"Let's go," she said.

She was silent all the way. We reached Indira hostel and she got in briskly without saying anything.

I moved to my hostel having all those moments of hugging and its upcoming consequences in future. I narrated everything to Robin.

"Boss you have now fifty-fifty chance of good and bad results but it will be decided by her only, so wait for her reaction," he said.

"It's difficult to wait yaar, I wish I should call her and apologize," I said.

"Are you mad? You didn't hug her, she did it, let her react first," Robin convinced me.

"I don't want to lose her, I must call her and apologize," I said and picked up my phone.

"You will not do it" Robin said and tried to snatch the phone from my hand. At once the phone rang.

Due to this pulling and tugging, the answer button got pressed and the call was received.

"Your call is on," Robin said.

"Without seeing the number I said, "Hello!"

"Hello... Raj, it's me Charu"

"Charu…" I said and looked at Robin.

Hearing her name Robin started dancing.

"I am sorry, I hugged you I shouldn't have done it," she said.

"Charu, I guess you feel I am close to you so you hugged me, what's wrong in it?" I said.

"I am not authorized to hug you," she said.

"Who is authorized then?" I asked.

"By which right I hugged you I don't know but it's true you are very close to me," she said.

"If you don't have any right on me I guess no girl on this earth has any right on me," I said.

"I hope you didn't mind it?" she said.

"No way Charu, why will I mind, it was the need of situation," I tried to convince her.

"Thanks Raj... I was worried, I don't want you to take me wrong," she said and the conversation ended.

"Why you were dancing behencho?" I asked.

"She called you by her own this is what I wanted, now I can say you have seventy thirty chance bro," he said.

"How much for positive result?" I asked.

"No doubt seventy for positive result" he said with confidence.

I didn't know how he used to be that much confident every time.

Time started running with its maximum speed. I and Charu kept meeting for short time now and then. Shivani used to visit our college now more frequently. It was the time when Rahul and Shivani came closer to each other. We several times caught them together at secluded place where I and Robin coincidently used to reach to ease our tension. Don't take us wrong we had not turned gay, but we used to go there to smoke and drink in a peaceful environment. We used to plan our life there in ecstasy of intoxication. I had no other topic except Charu and that rascal used to talk all the time none other than the girl he saw in Lagpat Nagar. It was not all about him, he did some more stupid acts to maintain his Rajput pride. Soon second year exams knocked our peaceful world and again we started working for it like a donkey. No need to say cigarettes were our weapon against the stress. Again Robin was free of stress as this year too his mind was engaged with a lady and it was more unfortunate condition as he did not know anything about that girl. Charu too started working hard to maintain her position. How hard it can be I felt when I was preparing to maintain my marks. Topping an exam is a tedious job. You don't need to work hard but also need luck. She used to call rarely these days and a couple of times when we met I saw her face all without glow, smile and intoxicating gestures. Any way exams passed and our campus was now stress -free and students started planning for their vacations. For me it was a bit difficult to be happy as I was going to be apart from Charu. Soon after her exam we met and she informed that she was going to Kolkata. This time she promised me to call from there as soon as she gets her number activated.

Monsoon hit India perhaps Kolkata first and then Bihar. We used to talk long even on STD calls which used to be very costly those days. I used to have sometimes a scarcity of money but all credit goes to mom who always gave me money to recharge my mobile. For the first time I liked the rain. I used to be under rain thinking love pearls are dropping from heaven and I should collect as much as possible to enrich myself. I knew Charu loved rain so I start liking rain and it started soothing me as romance has no bounds in this season. Our time passed well at home and time for starting a new year came.

# How to propose to your senior?

$W$e reached our respective hostels at the same date. Many guys were still at their homes. Robin was to come few days later. It feels really very bad after coming from home. In the evening I got a phone call from Charu.

"So what are you doing?" she asked.

"Nothing just trying to get out of home's hangover" I said.

"Ya me too," she said.

"What's your plan by the way for this evening?" she asked.

"Yet not decided" I said.

"Ok if you decide something, do inform me," she said.

"Ya... Sure"

I was lying on the bed and thinking about Charu. The pain was now unbearable for me. I hadn't proposed to her as yet as Robin had asked me not to do and also I waited very much for a suitable time, and in this way I lost many good chances. Having friendship with a senior girl was always ok but how much being in love with a senior girl is justified I didn't know. But I always knew I can't be happy without her love as I never tried for her friendship. I was worried if I will propose her and she may not like it then she may stop talking with me. It always frightened me. In between someone knocked at my door.

"It's open, come in," I said lying on the bed.

The door first opened a little and then completely. I looked at the doorway in suspense.

"Hi..." Charu entered the room and said.

I exclaimed, "You?"

I looked at the upper half of my body which was naked. She understood my situation and turned back.

"Don't you wear clothes in your room?" she angrily said.

"No... I mean yes, normally I do wear but it's very hot today and I never dreamt a girl will come to my room," I replied.

"Where's your shirt?" she asked.

"There, on that chair," I pointed towards a chair where a shirt was hanging.

She picked it and gave it to me turning her head in the opposite direction.

"Are you wearing trousers or you need that too?" she asked sarcastically.

"I am wearing trousers, thank you," I said.

"I was not expecting you here so I was like how guys be in their hostels," I explained.

"Its ok even girls too live like this in their hostels," she said and smiled.

"I knew you can not plan the evening so I thought to come to you as my room mate is also at home" she added.

"What a mess your room is in," she exclaimed looking around.

"How you live here?" she added and looked at me.

"Is this dirty? I thought it doesn't need a cleaning before two months," I replied

"But you should not have come in my room at this time," I said.

"Why? Don't you want me to come to your room?" she asked.

"It's not that but you know these guys will make an issue which will keep the campus abuzz the next couple of months at least," I explained.

"Oh I don't care" she said and looked around and walked about in the room.

Suddenly my sight went to the almirah where a few small posters of half naked models in Kamasutra pose were decorating its door.

"This rascal will leave me with no girl" I mumbled.

I ran towards the almirah which was about to be approached by Charu.

"Why don't you sit, nothing is here," I said and opened the door of the almirah quickly in order to get it out of her sight.

"Oh my God... It's a mess inside. Are these your clothes?" she looked at the almirah and exclaimed.

"Yes... Not just mine," I stammered.

"Do you wear them?" she asked.

"Definitely..." I replied.

"How can you keep them like this, these are not organized at all and even most of them are dirty," she said and looked at me turning up her nose.

"Don't you people wash them ever?" she asked.

"We do but not frequently" I scratched my head and replied.

"You guys are just impossible. When you come to meet a girl no one can imagine you live in such an unhygienic atmosphere," she said.

"You opened the door to hide something but I guess outside is at least better than inside so close the door and let these rags be in peace inside," she said and turned towards my bed.

I heaved a sigh of relief but no way, my sight went now to underwear hanging which was just to embarrass me. I again ran and collected it and threw it back. My life for a while became out of control.

"It is ok yaar, it's your room so why you are in such panic?" she said and smiled.

"My presence has upset you, I should have informed you of my coming," she said.

"No problem Charu, actually it is my first time with a girl in such solitude and I am a bit worried if somebody will see you here then you will become a part of gossip which may affect you," I said.

"I really like caring attitude, any way let's move out for dinner," she said.

"Ya that will be better," I said.

"Then get dressed," she said.

I kept standing for a while she looked at me and said "What happened, get dressed"

"Oh... I am sorry I will wait outside," she said and left.

I came out and we planned to have our dinner at Subhash canteen. I ordered non -veg for me but to my surprise Charu was a pure vegetarian.

"So you like non -veg?" she asked.

"No... I love non- veg, you can say till today this is my girl friend," I said.

"Oh that's great," she said.

"How can you be a pure vegetarian? Are you really from Kolkata?" I asked.

"Ya I am really from Kolkata and a pure vegetarian. Both contradictory?" she asked.

"I don't know but I have heard people there love fish and can't live without it?" I said.

"Ya it is true but not true for all," she said and smiled.

"How will you manage if your husband will be a non- vegetarian?" I asked.

"Very simple, I will tell him that I don't like it so you better leave it too," she smiled and said.

"Do you think he will leave?" I asked fearfully.

"Certainly yes if he loves me, if not then he will not," she said.

"Do you think it is justified?" I asked.

"Ya I think it is, as there may be a problem in future with this stupid non –veg," she said.

"Are you planning for a love marriage as you said he will love you he will leave it?" I asked.

"What's wrong if someone falls in love with me and I opt for love marriage but if I will not be that much lucky then also same condition will be for an arranged monkey," she said and laughed.

"What about you? Will you leave it if your wife or would- be will be a pure veg and she keeps a same condition before you?" she asked.

I was busy with the chicken's leg as I heard her question my mouth stopped masticating the soft tasty chicken inside my mouth, I looked at the leg piece which was in my hand and not very distant from my mouth and then I looked at Charu.

"Ya... Ya definitely I will leave if the girl will promise me to love me her whole life," I said in haste, and looking at the piece in my hand kept it back in the plate.

"I am sorry my tasty girl friend but it was the demand of situation as I have to impress the girl before me anyhow," I thought in my mind and kept looking at the piece longingly.

"You may carry on as for the time being your girl has not put forward any condition," she said and laughed.

"Oh ya..." I again picked it and started eating it.

"What is your feeling of being in love with some one?" I asked.

"Love is good... I mean if you find someone really worth it makes life beautiful," she said.

"I thought you must not be positive about love," I said.

"Why? Am I not a human being?" she asked.

"You are a topper, you work hard and generally these people don't waste their time in such activities" I explained.

"Any one can be a topper by virtue of hard work and luck but being a good human being is difficult, I think every body needs love and care," she said.

"Have you set any criteria of your dream man?" I asked.

"No... Certainly not but he must be you know mature enough to handle me," she said.

I didn't get her but I didn't dare to ask anything more.

"No one has proposed me so far?" she said and laughed artificially.

"No one? How is it possible?" I said being surprised.

"Ya, I guess guys think I am the serious type and not worth proposing," she said and looked at me.

I didn't say anything.

"Have you ever fall in love?" she asked.

I was surprised with her question.

"No so far but ya I have begun to like someone," I said.

"Good yaar... Who is she? Can I help you?" she exclaimed.

"Ya you can help, I will tell you some day," I said.

"Why someday why not today, I am eager to know the lucky girl," she said.

"Not today... I guess Saturday is my best day and I will propose her that day only and you will know everything," I said.

"Saturday is far away... I can't wait anymore," she said.

"Think about me ——how I waited for any positive sign from her," I said.

"So please don't ask me before Saturday as it is a question of my life," I requested.

"OK... lets wait for that day but if you need my help, you can call me anytime," she said.

"For your information I tell you a fact that she is my senior?" I said.

"What? Are you mad?" she exclaimed.

"How you will propose a senior and why should she accept it?" she said.

"I don't know. I love her so I must propose her and I should leave rest to her and God," I said.

"You are really crazy, I never knew this side of your nature," she said and put her hand on her head.

"Anyway I wish you good luck but the task is near impossible," she said.

"I know but I really need your good wishes," I said.

I dropped her at her hostel and came back to my hostel thinking all the way about her and how I should propose to her. Next day Robin came and I discussed everything with him.

"Now you don't have any option except proposing to her as you have already told her on Saturday you are going to propose to that girl" Robin said.

"If you will propose she will know the girl's name automatically and if not then she will compel you to say the girl's name and then too she will know, so better to be a man and propose to her as a man," Robin said toughly.

# Propose her on phone if you lack courage

"I am scared Robin, as she herself said it is near impossible," I said looking tensed.

"She told it is near impossible but didn't say it is absolutely impossible," Robin consoled.

"Ok I will propose to her day after tomorrow," I said.

The day came and I was nervous as hell. I was not able to do anything. I was in class but mentally I was preparing myself for my first love mission. After class Robin, Rahul and I went to the canteen for lunch.

"Robin I am very nervous, I am not able to collect the courage," I said sounding disappointed.

"It happens but you don't have any other option and think what if she says yes," Robin said.

"But what if she says 'No' and stops talking with me?" I said.

"Raj you love her, you never wanted her as a friend only, if she says yes you will have everything which you ever dreamt of and if she says no then most probably she may stop talking to you, in any case you don't need her friendship" Rahul said.

Rahul words somewhat boosted me but again shortage of courage was a problem.

Suddenly Charu with a few of her friends entered the canteen. She took a table not far from mine. She saw me and greeted me from there. My heart poked all of a sudden.

She soon finished her lunch and was going to her class. On the way when she came near to me, she gestured something with her hands without being unnoticed. I looked down and she felt as I hadn't seen her. She came near to me.

"Its Saturday, I hope you haven't forgotten, will you tell me her name?" she asked softly.

"I didn't forget, but Saturday is still far away," I said nervously.

"Ok, but don't forget, you have to tell me," she said and left.

"Robin did you see how nervous I was? How will I tell her it is none other than she?" I said.

"Ya I noticed but you have already put your head into the mortar." he said.

I cursed that bastard.

"Robin I can't propose to her on her face," I said."

"Then how will you do it?" he asked.

"I think I will do it over phone" I replied.

"Are you mad? It will not send a good message" Robin said and Rahul supported him.

"I don't know if I can do it in a conventional way. I am not a Rajput you know" I said.

They tried to convince me but I didn't listen to them and we were getting late for class too.

It was 4 o' clock. Every passing second made me more nervous.

"Robin I am going to propose her over phone" I said.

"Are you asking or you are saying?" Robin asked.

"If you are all set to do what you want, why are you asking? Go and do what you want," Robin said sounding irritated.

"Robin it is difficult for me why don't you understand? She is senior," I said.

"Your point is not wrong, ok, do it on phone if you like it" Rahul said and convinced Robin.

"Wait, we all go together and call her from a public booth," Robin suggested.

We went to a public booth near Chandrashekhar hostel. I smoked a few cigarettes in order to boost myself but it was not helping. It was now 5 o' clock and now I entered in booth leaving them outside.

I dialed Charu's number.

"Hello... Who is this?" Charu said.

"Hello... Charu... It's me .... Raj," I stammered.

"Raj... why haven't you called from your number? What happened?" she said anxiously.

"Actually I don't have balance so I am calling you from a booth," I stammered.

"What happened, are you alright?" she asked.

"I am not alright, I was never alright," I said.

"What happened, that girl turned down your proposal?" she asked.

"No... I didn't propose to her yet," I informed.

"Then why you are low pitched and when you will tell me her

name?" she asked.

"Charu, I am going to tell you her name?" I said.

"Ok tell me but you are so nervous even in telling me her name, how will you propose to her?" she asked.

"Charu, I don't know it is right or wrong but I am doing what I think is right," I said.

"Ya you should do whatever you think is right," she said.

"I can't hide it any more because as long as I will hide it my feelings will get more intense," I said.

"Ok yaar...Tell me at least and I promise if I can help you I will," she said.

"Your words encourage me enough to tell you her name," I said.

"It is none other than you Charu," I said collecting all my courage.

Suddenly the conversation ceased. We both became silent.

"Charu, if I have hurt you I am sorry but I was suffering a lot in hiding my feelings for you," I stammered.

"I know it is not normal as you are my senior but love has no limits, it can be for any one," I added.

She was listening without saying anything.

"For me it is you with whom I would like to spend the rest of my life," I said.

"I am not in hurry, you can take your time and I will have no complains either way," I added.

"Today I feel relaxed as there is no conflict between my mind and heart which used to torment me," I said.

"I have had a great time with you and for this life it is enough but as I am a human being I need you in my life," I said.

"I love you... now if you can help me please help me in achieving my love," I added.

"I don't know how I should react but as I promised to help you I will think about it," she stammered.

"Are you in hurry to know my answer?" she asked.

"No...Take your time" I stammered.

"Don't worry I will not keep you waiting long," she said.

Our conversation ended, I came out narrated everything to my friends and went to have tea and discuss this current issue.

# Girls' stupid questions after proposal: Concept of trial love

A few days later Charu called me on my number. She wanted to meet me at the old library which was situated at a dead end of the campus. Perhaps it was the Day of Judgment. I was sure of a refusal but I couldn't escape from it. This used to be the most secluded place of our medical world. Administration was planning a hostel there but for the time being it was just a place where anyone can have any privacy of any sorts. I had read somewhere that creations come out of solitude but this sort of a solitude was frightening. There was an ancient Ram temple which had never attracted anyone. I saw Charu sitting there. Her scooty was parked nearby.

"Why you chose this place?" I asked.

"Don't you fear this most secluded place?" I added.

"I don't know actually. I guess no other place will be as private as it is, and where I could be so comfortable" she said looking around.

"So how are you?" I asked.

"I guess I am fine but I was never been so confused in my life," she said.

"I really don't want to hurt you but I feel sometimes we should think for ourselves before anyone in life," she said placing her hand on her scooty's mirrors.

My heart beat became faster as now it was all except her acceptance. My ears became hot and it was hard for me to stand anymore. I moved from there and sat on the stairs of the temple.

She came to me and sat by my side.

"Are you OK?" she asked.

"Ya... I am fine, carry on," I stammered.

"Since when do you love me?" she asked.

"When I met you the second time," I said.

"Is falling in love with a senior OK for you?" she asked.

"I really don't have any idea, but hiding and suppressing one's love is not ok" I said.

"Why do you love me?" she asked.

I don't know why girls don't have common sense. I was not expecting such a stupid question. I had no answer but not answering a question will develop any doubt in her mind so I opted to answer.

"One doesn't fall in love with any purpose, perhaps one thinks no one can be better than the person with whom he has fallen in love," I tried my best to convince her with my answer.

"Do you know no one has dared to propose me so far, although many like me?" she said.

I was silent. I really had no idea whether she was telling me a fact or scolding me?

"What do you want to be in future?" she asked.

"A surgeon of course, but only being a surgeon will not give me satisfaction," I said.

"Then what will give you all the satisfaction?" she asked.

"I want to join Rashtriya Swayam Sewak Sangh and want to do something for my country," I said.

"Ok so you are a Sanghi?" she asked giving me a tough look.

"I am proud to be a Sanghi," I said.

"Will this of my plan affect your decision?" I asked

"No, not at all. I think this is a democratic country and every one is free to do what he thinks is good" she said looking around.

I heaved a sigh of relief. We sat there for long and discussed many boring topics but not a single word about her decision. I was restless to know my fate.

"So... what have you decided?" I asked suddenly.

"A conflict is still in my mind" she said scratching her forehead.

"Do you need more time?" I asked.

"My brain suggests me to turn down your proposal and my heart says to give it a try," she said in confusion.

"Being in love with a junior will tarnish my image and is not good for my reputation," she added.

"OK... I got it, you are turning down," I said.

I stood up and as I tried to walk away she held my hand and said, "I didn't say that, I was telling you about the conflict."

"I didn't reveal what I am saying on it," she said with a smile.

"I am saying what's wrong being in love with a junior, let's give it a chance but I want to tell you I am not accepting your proposal," she said.

I looked confusedly at her.

"Let's be in a relationship like all normal couples but unlike them you will not be privileged to be intimate with me," she said in one breath.

"I mean to say let's check each other as a partner and if it works we can continue for ever," she said.

"If it will not work we will be apart and if it will work then we will be like all normal couples but unlike them I will not be privileged to be intimate with you for ever or what?" I tried to know the condition.

"This condition is just for the time being to check each other" she said and smiled.

"Have you planned to be intimate with me?" she asked naughtily.

I didn't say anything. She came to me, hugged me and whispered in my ears "Congrats."

"So the deal is done now. We will be in a relationship for the time being and will check each other and if it will work we will continue or will part" she said.

"One more thing, I can be intimate with you when I want but not you," she said.

I was totally clueless about what she was suggesting? I was confused whether I should be happy for getting my love temporarily or should be sad for all the crap she was suggesting. It was like a chicken leg piece which is near me and yet I can't eat it no matter how hungry I am. It was no less than a cruel joke that, that chicken piece can come closer, can dance on my lips but I can't take in. She dropped me at Kabir hostel and as usual I discussed everything with Robin. This concept of trial love was strange to him too.

# Crush became crash: What if your dream girl is your proff?

I and charu were just on a trial. I had no apprehension in my mind but she wanted to judge me. My love affair was not normal at all as I was in love with a senior. I and Charu used to be together after our classes most of the time. Every one now started speculating that there is something fishy between us. I was trying hard to convince Charu that I am her real soul mate and there something was just to rock Robin's world.

Love is a gift of god which comes in our way suddenly and it has no limitations. We were then in 3rd year. We had to attend a lecture of obstetrics. We were asked by the administration to be in obstetrical ward by 9 AM. Robin was so punctual that we reached there by 8:15.

"Now what Robin?" I asked.

"Why we came here so early?" I added with irritation.

"Its our first class so I didn't want to be late, come lets visit this department" he said pulling my hand.

"I am not interested, better you visit this dead department where I can't find anybody"

"Ok then why don't you talk to charu on phone and pass your time" he advised with a teasing tone and walked from there. I called charu on phone and started passing my time as charu was also a puzzle for me. She used to act and ask me to do what I had never imagined in my life. I didn't have any experience of trial love.

After 10 minutes he came back with a glowing face. He was very happy and restless.

"What happened Robin?" I asked.

"Come with me" he said and made me run behind him.

We reached to another side of that building.

"What you want to show me?" I asked being irritated.

"Look this car" he said and pointed towards a red brown car.

"What's unique in this car, this is not the single Chevrolet" I said.

"Behencho.. look at number plate" he said in excitation.

I read the number it seemed familiar.

"This number seems familiar to me" I said in confusion.

"This can be familiar to you but it is not less than a life line for me" he said.

"Oh my God if I am not wrong this is the number of the girl's car whom you saw in Lagpat Nagar" I exclaimed.

"You are absolutely right now this is proved that my love for her is very strong and she has any connection with me" he said being confident.

"She must be around, I should find her and today I will not let her go without expressing my love for her" he said and moved towards cafeteria.

He came again in ten minutes with a disappointed face.

"Now what happened? Did you find her" I asked.

"I saw her in cafeteria, as I saw her I lost somewhere and as I came back in my sense she was not there" he said. I looked at robin's face which was grief struck.

"Don't worry she will come to you as she came today perhaps god is testing you" I tried to consol him.

"I saw her today almost after six months I can't wait another six month even I do have a heart which is dying every moment for her" he said in grief.

"Raj you want to see me happy? If yes then believe me if she will be in my life I will be very content and happy" he said with a confidence.

As some where I was responsible for his broken heart so I just prayed to god, there must not be anything bad with Robin this time.

The lecture hall was all packed and noisy. Students were busy in their regular topic about sex and girls and newly discovered porn sites and videos. A girl entered in lecture hall. She was in blue jeans and a tight pink top. Her untied hairs were flying; she had wearing a bracelet from the circumference violet pearls were hanging. All features of her face and body were demanding, full of intoxicating youth.

Every one stared staring at her with typical hungry male eyes. Every one left discussing porn for a while and sank in that beauty and soon lecture room flooded with moaning.

"Students.....please keep quite" she said.

There was no decrement in noise level.

"keep silence …. I said… I am your teacher" she shouted at us.

Now it was a command and everyone became silent with their

mouth wide open with a great surprise. As she entered class room Robin face turned red and he started breathing fast it seemed he underwent hypoxia. I could hear his breaths.

Robin was upset and in that way he hit the desk. It was a pin drop silence and every body including madam started looking at Robin.

"You….. man in black T shirt….. what's your problem?

It was our first day and it was going to be bad for Robin.

"maam actually I did it in frustration" he stood and replied.

"Frustration? I didn't get you" she said giving a dirty look.

"Maam you are very young and you are our teacher. Isn't it frustrating?"

Every one cracked into laughter. She stared us and all silent once again.

"What's your name?" she asked.

"Robin Raman Singh" he said again with that rajpooti attitude.

"In front of me, you are just a kid Robin… so don't stress your mind and be ready for a hectic ward duty and subject" she cleared her intentions in one simple sentence.

"My name is Ankita Srivastva… I am MS obstetrics and I will teach you basic obstetrics"

"I already met one of your crazy friends and I am also not interested in your introduction, so better start our basic theme of the day"

"You must be familiar with female's genital organs as we will deal with these organs in this subject"

Again class became noisy with a mere introduction of this word 'genitalia'.

"No need to imagine much and don't make this class a fish market as you will never do vaginal examinations" she added.

Suddenly our over excitement eloped leaving us with a great disappointment. Many of us were thinking to get an opportunity of such practical.

She gave us basic information about female's genitalia which was all ready known to us. I noticed robin didn't blink his eyes even once during lecture.

When lecture finished we didn't know as her presence made the class room a fairy land which we had seen in our childhood dreams.

We came out and I asked Robin "why you got overexcited in class?"

"Will you believe me…. This is the girl whom I saw first in Lajpat Nagar and then today in cafeteria" he said with frustration.

"OH no Robin….its not possible yaar" I said.

"Ya that I know but you know me , I cant withdraw myself" he replied with tough look.

"What you are going to do?" I asked in fear.

"Nothing much… but definitely I will propose her some day" he said with stretched face.

"There are only two ways, either she accept me or kick my ass, choice is hers" he added.

Now it was clear to me that something unusual is going to be in college as I was very much aware of his intensions. It was impossible to convince Robin so I even didn't try.

Life at this was totally different. I had no time for study and cricket. Rahul used to leave college as the final bell used to ring. I didn't notice him very much but it seemed he used to wait for the final bell to ring since he used to step in college. Robin too had become entirely different. We three didn't get time to sit together and when I and robin used to be together, he used to be lost and perhaps me too. I noticed robin playing with paper and pen. I guessed he want to do better in Obstetrics to impress Ankita madam. What's wrong in it every body should do anything to get his love. Robin's behavior was different but it seemed me normal as he became a bit disciplined. Love teaches you many things and helps you to be oriented.

# Pregnancy: A disease?

Our obstetric class was at peak as Ankita madam was really a good teacher but a teacher can't do better if students are not willing to study. Like me every student was really not interested in obstetrics unlike me every student was interested in ma'am.

"Today we will discuss diagnosis of pregnancy" Ankita ma'am said and wrote it in bold letters at board.

"Without planning Pregnancy is just a disease"

"Now-a-days tradition is quite different, pregnancy before marriage is quite common and reports say near about every sixth girl becomes pregnant before marriage, it is not of our interest but our interest is to confirm and diagnose the pregnancy" she said.

"Being a doctor you must know the signs of pregnancy"

"So who can give me a detail of signs of pregnancy?" she asked.

I hid myself behind the back of a student. A few hands were in air to answer. She chose Suneet the scholar of our batch.

"Ma'am signs are like amenorrhoea, Chadwick's sign…" madam interrupted him.

"This is not the right way of answering, any one else"

All the hands disappeared from air and a new hand attracted every body's attention even ma'am was surprised with this new presence.

"Can I try ma'am?" it was robin who asked.

"Yes Robin sure, I am really happy that you are still in class unlike your other good friends" ma'am said and gave us a bad look.

"Ma'am signs of pregnancy have been divided in two groups 1 subjective i.e. amenorrhoea, morning sickness, vomiting etc (2) objective i.e. breast changes, chadwick's sign, vaginal sign etc" he described everything like an expert.

I was really jealous of Robin. How that rascal studies this boring subject? Then again like a looser I consoled myself by saying "It is all to impress the lady, I am not interested so I don't study"

This was the first time when robin was noticed for his intellect by every one including ma'am. Since that day robin started doing better and better and in this subject even scholars couldn't dare to challenge him. There was something peculiar which I noticed in Ankita madam, now she was paying attention at robin. The obstetrics class became a film for me, in which I can notice a hidden romance between a female professor and one of her student. Robin used to look at Ankita ma'am fearlessly and continuously. I noticed Ankita madam was aware of robin's daring act and for my surprise I noticed ma'am looking at Robin with corner of her eyes several times. For me it became a good time pass.

If by chance you get a female teacher and too very beautiful and young, you can't imagine the level of student's fantasy. Ankita madam's bold beauty became a topic of discussion for every body from class room to canteen. Vulgar imagination of students for her used to kick my mind. It is quite common at place like medical college.

We were waiting for our proff in dermatology class. One guy was playing his FM radio. Romantic songs from that radio were creating a romantic wave which was at its ecstasy without the proff.

"It is Radio mirchi and we are announcing a fashion competition for every one if you have a talent to design a dress or anything related to this you can send your entries to us. Tomorrow is last day of entry, so hurry up send us your entries as soon as possible"

Proff was very late today. Robin went out of the class and I put out my phone and started chatting with Charu on yahoo from class itself. She used to be online sometimes from class and when she used to be she used to give me a miss call. I tell you life is just a hell without internet and mobile.

# Trial Love: I was in air

Few days later again I and charu were chatting from our respective classes.

"What you are doing?" she wrote.

"Nothing just a boring class of preventive medicine, what you are doing"

"My class is going to over, if your class is really boring come for a lunch with me within ten minutes in Subhas's canteen" she wrote.

"How I can come? I am in class. Can we have a lunch after my class?" I asked.

"No I am going out today for shopping with my friends so you will have to come in ten minutes" she wrote.

"How?" I wrote.

"I don't know if you want you will have to come within ten minutes so don't waste your time and manage to come anyhow" she wrote and logged off.

"Fuck.. how I will reach there in just ten minutes" I mumbled.

Rahul looked at me with inquisition and asked "What happened?"

"I have to reach subhas canteen anyhow within ten minutes" I said.

"Class will continue for an hour still" he said.

"That I know but I have to, you know I am on trial only she didn't accept yet" I replied.

"It seems quite impossible to leave as proff will not let you go" he said.

"Tell the last guy in row to open the window" I said looking at window.

"What you are going to do?" Rahul asked giving me a dirty look.

"I will jump out from there" I said.

"Behencho are you mad? We are at 1st floor idiot, it can damage your bones" he scolded.

"I know but I have to" I said and through crossing all the legs below desk I reached at last guy near the window.

"You have also become an erratic living with that rascal Robin" he said.

I tapped his legs and asked him to open the window. I asked him to give me a signal when proff will be busy writing something at board. As he signaled me I climbed up and jumped without thinking anything. For a few seconds I was in air and my heart was just to come out of my mouth. I realized for the first time that it's not the height but the fear which takes the life first.

Thanks god the land over which I placed myself was a bit muddy due to yesterday night rain. I anyhow collect myself and ran away from there. My cloths were all dirty, it seemed as someone has dropped me into a gutter. I had no time to change my cloths so I reached subhas canteen with dirty cloths and pain which I got in order to jump. Pain started increasing with every moment.

I saw charu sitting with her friends as I came nearer her friends left her and occupied another tables.

"What happened to your cloths?" she asked.

"Nothing I just jumped from 1ˢᵗ floor so it got dirt" I replied

"So you will have your lunch with these cloths?" she asked.

"No option you had asked me to reach here within ten minutes, changing cloths could have made me late" I said.

"Take your seat" she said pointing chair in front of her.

Almost every body looked at me and perhaps whispered about my dirty cloths and my foolishness. It was difficult to eat but I pretended to eat.

"Have you thought something about my proposal?" I asked.

"About your proposal? When you proposed me?" she said and looked at me.

"A month ago on phone, don't you remember?" I asked.

"Was that the way to propose? Propose me traditionally" she said smiling.

"Stop kidding Charu" I said being a bit annoyed.

"No I am serious propose me like everyone does, having a red rose in your hand, kneeling down"

"Do it today and now I start thinking on it" she added.

"Get a flower, come to back side of this building and propose me there, no body will see you proposing me" she said.

"Are you serious?" I asked.

"I am damn serious" she confirmed.

I had no choice than leaving the table and getting a red rose for such an idiotic way of proposal. I was cursing the man who formulated this tradition. We had five rose stall in our campus only so getting a rose was not a problem. I came back to the building. Charu was sitting under a big statue of Jawahar lal Nehru. I came near.

"So are you ready to propose me?" she said.

I nodded my head in confirmation.

"Ok do it" she said in loud pitch.

"Charu, this is a truth that marriage is fixed from heaven but we try hard to get the special one here on Earth as soon as possible I think you are the one for me with whom I would like to spend rest of my life. Please accept my proposal and be mine" I thus proposed.

As my proposal ended I heard some whispering from other side of statue. Suddenly a bunch of girls came from other end having a recorder in a girl's hand. They looked at me and started shouting. One of them even pointed her finger to that recorder.

"You said no body will see me proposing here, but how come your friends were hiding here?" I asked being disappointed.

"You proposed me, I will now think on it, no further questions" she said and ran fast to join her friends and then collected that recorder. Needless to say it was great blow to my sentiments. I returned my hostel with a heavy heart. Charu became more puzzled day by day as she was asking me to do the things which I had never imagined but I didn't lose my determination to get her in my life so I tried doing what she used to ask me.

# Birthday became campus buzz

A few weeks later on the eve of 10th September, I saw Robin very restless. He came to me and asked me to come along with him to South Ex.

"Why this sudden shopping Robin?" I asked.

"Don't tell me you are not coming with me" he said.

"I will certainly come with you, but why you are that restless?" I asked.

"I will tell you every thing but later don't ask me when" he said.

I dressed myself and we reached South Ex II. We parked the bike.

"Listen Raj.. if you don't want to come wait here only because I will take time" he said.

"Better you wait here and guard our bike and pass your time by chatting as you do now-a-days" he said, smiled and went.

"Bloody fucker have I come here to guard this bike?" I shouted at him but he didn't mind.

I logged inn to yahoo and I saw Charu on line. I sat near a Chaat thela and started chatting. I tell you I used to chat every day the same fucking things like what are you doing? How was your day? And at last have you thought anything regarding my proposal? Needless to say every day the same fucking old answers used to chop my heart, but it is love you will have to do anything for getting a positive answer. After an hour Robin came back carrying a big poly beg which was tightly packed. I could not guess the stuffs inside.

"What is in this beg?" I asked.

"You will know later and stop asking me such fucking questions can't you do anything without inquisition" he said being irritated.

"Behencho.. Inquisition is the mother of invention but if you don't want to say I will not ask but tell me what I have to do with this beg?" I asked

"Why you use the wrong quotations? You have to carry this beg all the way without tempering beg and keeping your mouth shut" he said and started the bike with a kick.

I sat all the way keeping my mouth shut but I tried a lot to temper beg in order to see the stuffs inside but that rascal had packed it very carefully with three poly begs. He stopped the bike near a staff quarter not far from our hostel.

"Give me this beg and sit here only, I am just coming" he took beg from me and went inside. After ten minutes he came out with a man who seemed familiar but I was totally confused where I saw him. They exchanged few words with smile and then Robin came back. I was looking at him with some suspicion.

"Why you are looking at me that way?" he asked.

"Your behaviors today are totally different you are doing nonsense today like before but difference is that you are not telling me anything about your stupidity today" I said being angry.

"Don't be angry darling, you will know everything later" he said and drove the bike towards hostel.

We had our dinner together and then robin came to me and said "Raj.. I am going out, tonight I will not be at room so don't worry, where I am going don't ask me as you…"

I interrupted him in between and completed his sentence "As I will know everything later"

"Ya darling" he smiled and said.

"I am worried about you as you are doing really something nonsense" I shouted.

"Don't worry, I will be fine and I am doing what I think is right, you will know everything tomorrow" he said, collected his college beg and bike key and moved out.

Next day we had obstetrics class. As I entered the class room, my mouth became wide open to see the walls of the class. Not a single inch of class wall was left by the colored paper. All the walls were decorated by the colored paper and plastics. It was looking a party hall not a class room. I saw the students around in order to clear my doubt that really this is my class room or I have entered in a wrong room.

"What is all this?" I asked

"Can't you read the sentences on the colored paper… illiterate person" one of them said and all started laughing.

"HAPPY BIRTHDAY TO YOU MA'AM" I read.

"Whose birthday?" I asked.

"Ankita madam's" one told among them.

"Fuckers you don't have another business except this" I said and took my seat.

Ma'am entered in class room and she became stupefied when she saw the walls. She read perhaps every colored paper on which anything was written. As she finished the last paper a few students stood up and sprinkled room fresheners and fumes and every body stood up and wished ma'am by singing the traditional song of birthday. Ma'am at once latched the door and shouted "Stop it.. I said Stop it"

Suddenly every body kept quite.

"Who did all this?" she asked in anger.

Every body turned towards Robin. I was totally surprised.

"So you did it all Robin?" ma'am asked.

"Yes ma'am, it was your birthday so I thought to give you a surprise as.."

Ma'am interrupted him in between and shouted at him "Shut up, I have never expected any such surprises from any body"

"Who asked you to show your stupidity?" she added.

Robin bowed his head. I looked at Robin with great sympathy.

"I beg you people don't do such things and don't make my problems more complicated" she said.

"Just remove all the papers from the wall right now" she ordered.

Robin moved toward the walls. I and Rahul tried to assist him but he stopped us to do that. I was looking at him continuously and he was tearing all the papers with trembling hands and watery eyes. I cursed madam for such a bad reaction. Now I got what Robin did all yesterday night. In mere twenty minutes wall became as ugly as it used to be every day. Robin collected all the papers and stuff and threw it in a dust bean near by.

Ma'am went out of room and Robin unintentionally followed her. Ma'am was standing in corridor and she cracked in tears. Robin looked her for few minutes and then went near her. As she noticed robin coming to her she tried to hide her tears.

"Ma'am I am really very sorry, I didn't have any intention to hurt you but I am really an erratic as my friends say" he stammered.

"Robin go to class, I am just coming and forget all these things for ever" she said.

Robin came back to class and collected one more poly bag and moved towards dust bean. Ma'am entered then only and asked "What is in this poly bag?"

"Nothing ma'am just a cake, but of no use so I am sending it to dust bean" robin said.

"Keep this on this table" ma'am said pointing towards a table by the side of lecture box.

Robin kept it there and took his seat between me and Rahul. Ankita ma'am looked Robin for long time and then started day's topic. After class when all students were to leave the class, Ankita madam asked us to stay for sometimes.

"Don't you people want me to cut the cake?" she asked.

"Every body except Robin shouted "yes madam".

She went near the table where cake was kept and then turned back and looked at Robin.

"Robin.. Come here" she said.

Robin was all silent and every body was looking at Robin and ma'am.

"Robin I am talking to you, come here" she said again.

I and Rahul pushed Robin and then Robin moved towards Ma'am unwillingly.

"I am going to cut the cake but don't make noise, admin doesn't consider it good and will send me so cause notice" she explained.

All agreed and nodded their head. Ma'am cut the cake and feed a piece to robin. Robin became emotional and looked at us with those watery eyes which were full of love for a special person standing by his side. We raised our thumbs up to wish him. He then feed a piece to ma'am and it looked very romantic but unusual one. I could co relate this with me as my romance was also an unusual one. Rest students just became jealous of Robin's fortune. This episode rocked the rest medicos and campus for another few weeks. Robin and I were the topic of discussion because of our ladies. People started speculating much about Robin and ma'am which were baseless for the time being.

# Destiny of soul mates: Parts I

One day we were in the Neurology department to make the reports of the newly admitted patients. I saw Rahul looking all tensed and he was making calls to someone continuously. After our ward duty we met at the lecture hall.

"Rahul.. what's wrong?" I asked.

"Whom were you making calls too so frequently?"

" Shivani Yaar," he said placing his head on the desk.

"Is every thing alright?" Robin asked.

"No yaar.. it was never alright but it was not as bad as it is this time," he said.

"You know Shivani's Asst. manager is a mother fucker. He always expresses his evil desires indirectly to Shivani several times but yesterday he proposed Shivani a promotion in lieu of spending one night with him."

Hearing this we both turned red with anger.

"I will kill that rascal, give me his number," Robin said angrily.

"Did Shivani tell you all this?" I asked.

"Yes, she told me and she has been crying since yesterday. I am calling her but she is not receiving my calls," he said sounding disappointed.

"You are a rascal Rahul, she wants you to understand her situation," Robin shouted at Rahul.

"What I can do yaar? I am confused." Rahul said.

"Why you are confused? Don't you love her?" he asked.

"I love her very much, I can die for her," Rahul said desperately.

"Don't die for her, live for her and make her live," Robin said.

Sometimes a stupid guy can also speak meaningfully. He dialed Shivani's number and talked to her.

"She is coming here, so be prepared to take some extraordinary decision," Robin said.

We missed lecture that day. Shivani came and we took all the information regarding this Assist manager. We left them alone and we went to our favorite smoking adda.

"Shivani, I am sorry for every thing, I never understood your feelings," Rahul said.

"I know you can have any good guy and a good life but your love for me is not allowing you those things," he stammered.

Shivani became emotional and burst into tears.

"Don't cry Shivani, my heart is melting," he said and hugged her tightly.

"I am not God but I promise you that I will never make you cry. I want to marry you as soon as possible," he said kissing Shivani on her forehead.

Suddenly tears started making their ways fast through her cheeks, lips and nose.

"This is what I longed for years, please make me yours for ever if you love me," she stammered.

"I love you and can't live without you," he said and kept his lips on hers.

They started kissing each other madly and suddenly clouds poured love over them in the form of rain. They ran towards a half -built hostel and stood in its lee. Shivani's long hair was dripping with water. Rahul came near to her and caught a drop between his lips and then pulled her and again kissed her. Two half wet bodies were on fire for a few minutes forgetting the rest of the world.

When the rain stopped, they came to us having holding each other's hands.

"So what's the deal?" Robin asked.

"The deal is for ever. We are going to marry," Rahul said confidently.

"What? Really?" I asked being surprised.

"Ya.. its already late, I know I am not earning now but some day I will earn too but for the time being Shivani will work," Rahul said.

I looked at Shivani, she was looking down but she was unable to hide her immense happiness. I hugged and congratulated her.

"But first you will have to take permission from your parents," I said looking at Rahul.

"And you too Shivani," I added.

"My mom is ok with my decision and she knows it. But I will seek her permission today," she said.

"I will tell every thing to my parents and I don't think they will have any problem accepting Shivani as their daughter in law," he said.

"I am there for you both my dear, ask me anytime for any help," Robin said.

We hugged them and congratulated them and wished them all the best. Rahul explained every thing to his parents and Shivani to her mother and the most important thing was that they both got positive response from their parents. Both side parents met and discussed every thing. People from both sides were very noble so not a single dispute arose and they took a collective decision of marriage next year by February. There was a small party on this occasion from both the sides; I and Robin were the first to be invited.

# A Pleasant surprise: A Fashion show

$1$0th October. We were in the obstetrics class. Robin looked very happy.

"Today you guys are coming with me to Le Meridian hotel," Robin said to me and Rahul.

"What's there?" we asked in unison.

"That is a secret. I can't tell you now," Robin said.

We had our routine class of obstetrics and when class was over Robin went to Ankita madam.

"Ma'am... One minute please," Robin said.

"Robin... I am busy right now, come to my office after an hour," ma'am said and went out.

After an hour Robin went to ma'am office and as he was to knock the door, he heard madam shouting at some one on the phone. He didn't knock but tried to hear the conversation at least from this side.

"I am not your slave; I will do whatever I would like"

"Cut this crap; don't try to be great, I know how great you are?"

"Just fuck off, I don't want to talk to you and listen you did what you liked now you can't stop me doing what I like," she said and ended the conversation.

Robin waited for few minutes and then knocked the door.

"Come in," ma'am said.

Robin entered the office and saw ma'am trying hard to wipe her tears in order to hide it from Robin.

"Ma'am I hope I am not disturbing you?" Robin stammered.

"No not at all Robin... Take your seat" Madam said pointing towards a chair.

"Ma'am I want to invite you for..." before he could complete ma'am interrupted him.

"Sorry Robin, I can't accept any invitation," she said rudely.

"Ma'am there is something in Le meridian hotel and I have a pass for you, without your presence every thing there will be useless," Robin pleaded.

"What is there? Have you again planned any surprise for me?" ma'am asked being tough.

"I can't say anything right now but I can definitely say without you everything will be just in vain" Robin said and forwarded the pass to ma'am.

Ma'am took the pass and looked it from both the sides. Nothing was written except VIP PASS and Hotel's name and function's floor.

"Nothing is written on it," ma'am said.

"If it was written I have not given it to you right now" he said.

"Ma'am there is a function there, at 8 o' clock evening so please come, I will be waiting for you," he said and stood up.

"Robin I am not promising you anything but there is a little chance of my coming," madam said, keeping pass in her purse.

"This world is existing just on chance and hope madam, let me hope for your arrival," he said and moved out of office.

We reached le meridian hotel at 7:30 evening and then at 10th floor. Floor was all decorated with beautiful posters. FASHION INDIAWELCOMES YOU TO FASHION DESIGN COMPETITION" it was written in bold letters at entrance.

Robin showed his pass to the security person and he allowed us to go in. I and Rahul were totally confused.

"Rascal from where you got this pass?" I asked.

"Shut up and follow me you fucker," Robin said and walked in.

On the wall few designs were hanging. Robin went near one of them and touched it.

"It is really very beautiful," both me and Rahul said in unison.

"This is not a design my friend but a hope, a love and life," Robin said and moved towards the auditorium.

The auditorium was packed with important people from different fields. We took our seat in the fourth row. Robin looked at his watch. He looked a bit disappointed. Soon a host appeared at the dais and said "Fashion India welcomes you on a great occasion of result of mega fashion competition, for your kind information we have received twenty thousand designs from non professional designers, and few of them are so deserving that they gave a tough challenge to professional's design and figured themselves in top five winning designs. Ladies and gentleman hold your breath for that time and enjoy some beautiful performance. Thank you"

Soon the stage was occupied with beautiful dancers. Robin again looked at his watch. It was 8:30. He seemed restless. Suddenly his mobile rang and he moved out talking on the phone. I watched him for a while but the beautiful dancers were more interesting than Robin for the time being. Rahul disturbed me by nudging my arm with his elbow.

"What happened ?" I asked.

"Look there, with whom Robin is coming," he said and pointed me to a direction with his eyes.

"O my God, its Ankita madam!" I exclaimed.

As they came near we stood up.

"Sit.. Sit.. So you two are also here," she said and took a seat. I was sitting with Rahul and then Robin and then Ankita ma'am. Between the performances, the host used to come to the stage to entertain and announce something. Robin and ma'am were talking but what they were talking I couldn't hear due to noise but it seemed everything was OK.

"Ladies and gentlemen our jury's verdict about the selection of the top five designs is now out and the fifth prize goes to Manish Rawal , a fashion designer. Put your hands together for Manish Rawal. Again he came after a performance and announced the winner's name whose design was ranked fourth and then third and it was now the time for the second prize.

"Ladies and gentlemen talent has no limitations, every one is talented, and the difference is that he or she doesn't know about it most of the time. It is perfectly true about the winner of our second prize. Can you imagine a hand which is being trained to save lives of people by treating their diseases can even make a design which not only challenged many designers' design but made them out of this race and placed itself on prestigious number two position?"

"Fashion India is pleased to announce the name of that young man, ladies and gentlemen please put your hands together for a medico and the promising designer of future Mr. Robin Raman Singh and I will request the lady to come on stage, whom he dedicated this design ——Miss Ankita Srivastva"

"It is a beautiful design of sari which has been accepted by a leading sari manufacturer and the first sample will be gifted to the lucky lady and the prize money of 70,000 rupees will be presented to Mr. Robin Raman. Please come on stage," the host announced.

Every body was giving applauds to Robin but three people were just wonder struck — me, Rahul and Ankita ma'am.

Robin stood up, tightened his tie and said, "Ma'am please come."

Ma'am somehow collected her poise which was just lost after the announcement and moved towards stage. They collected their respective gift and prize. Then the top winner's name was announced and we were asked to go to the dinner hall. We went there including Robin and ma'am.

"Is it really true that Robin has won a second prize in a reputed fashion competition?" I asked Rahul.

"It is hard for me to believe even but it is the only truth of the day," Rahul said helping himself to a dish.

"That fucker never told me that he had participated in any competition like this," I said angrily.

"No idea man, I didn't know how talented this guy is?" Rahul said.

I looked at Robin and Ankita ma'am exchanging words a few feet away. I could hear whatever they were talking.

"Robin let's go out," ma'am said.

"Ma'am its dinner time, are you getting late?" Robin asked.

"No... I want to have dinner outside somewhere else," she said.

"But where ma'am?" Robin asked.

"Let's go out and decide" she said.

Robin came to us and informed that he is going out with madam and he had no idea when he would come back. I and Rahul enjoyed the dinner at the five star hotel, forgetting everything. The evening was really very lucky for Robin and informative for us. It made us acquainted with one more hidden talent of Robin.

# India Gate: A little about the Past

Robin and ma'am came out of Le Meridian and were standing at its entrance.

"Ma'am where will we go?" Robin asked.

"I don't have any idea, but India Gate is not a bad idea," she said.

"Let's go there and have our dinner," she added.

Robin looked at ma'am with confusion as dinner at India Gate was a strange idea. There was no restaurant around it. Ma'am got into her car out of the parking yard and Robin got in and they drove to India Gate. Within ten minutes they were at India Gate, crossing Maan Singh Road. Ma'am stopped the car not far from the entrance. It was a cloudy night and a bit cold. Robin looked at his watch. It was 10 o' clock.

"Ma'am I guess there is no restaurant around, where we will have dinner?"Robin said.

"Ya, you are absolutely right, there is no restaurant here but I used to have dinner here five years ago very frequently," she said.

"No restaurant, but you used to have dinner here? I don't get you" Robin asked in confusion.

Suddenly ma'am ran towards a *thela* man shouting "Uncle.. Uncle!"

He was a sixty years old man, with full white hair and dirty clothes torn at several places. The *thela* man stopped and looked at Ma'am very keenly for long.

"Darpi uncle... Don't you recognize me?" she asked.

Robin walked towards *thela*. He came to them and stood silently.

"Your face is quite familiar but I am confused beti," thela man said.

"I am Ankita, don't you remember I used to come very often with my friend Vishal Agnihotri to your thela for dinner, those days you used to put your thela here only," she explained.

"Are you Ankita Srivastva?" That old man came nearer, looked at ma'am and asked.

"Yes uncle, I am Ankita Srivastva," she said with happiness.

"I don't put my *thela* here now as you know now-a-days these police men are not allowing and even demand good money for that" he said being disappointed.

"Uncle I was very fond of your chhola chawal, we have come here just hoping to have it from you," she said.

"Beti there is nothing left beside one plate of Chhola chawal, I guess it was for you, one man ordered but didn't come, but it will not be enough for two of you," old man said sadly.

"I am really very happy to see you after so long; you used to be a medical student those days. What are you doing now?" The old man asked.

"I am now a medical professor, I am teaching them obstetrics," madam said pointing at Robin.

"Obstet..?" old man could not pronounce the word.

"It is branch of medicine related with pregnancy and delivery," Robin tried to make him understand.

"Uncle please give us whatever is left, we are really very hungry," ma'am said.

"Where you will sit and have it?" he asked.

"Here only," ma'am said.

"Ankita... Police will come and fine me," he said sounding scared.

"Don't worry uncle I will pay the fine," Ma'am said.

The old man gave them a plate of chhola chawal. Ma'am collected the plate and sat on the grass not far from main road. Robin and the old man followed her. They all sat together. Ma'am asked Robin to eat offering her spoon. Robin hesitated but soon started eating. Ma'am was eating like she was hungry since years.

"Uncle even today, your chhola chawal has no match," ma'am said gulping a mouthful.

"Beti.. Where is your friend Vishal, you people were to marry?" he asked.

Ma'am had a boy friend, hearing this Robin became a bit upset.

"We could not marry uncle," ma'am said keeping her spoon on the dish.

She could not hold back her tears.

"Ma'am…" Robin couldn't say any more and offered his hanky to ma'am.

Ma'am soon wiped her tears and again started eating. The old darpi's fear was not baseless. Soon a police jeep stopped at his thela and shouted, "Whose thela is this? Where is the bloody thela man?"

Old darpi ran towards his thela saying "Sarkaar its mine"

"Rascal... why you parked your thela here, should I thrash you?" a police man was just about to thrash the old man.

"Hey officer wait... we had asked him to do that," Robin said walking to them.

"Are you a prime minister? Who will pay the fine?" one of them shouted at Robin.

"If I was a prime minister you will not fine me then? Or a fine will sew your mouth?" Robin asked.

"Saale.. Badi garmi hai kya? Yahi jhaad dunga," police man said and approached to Robin.

"What you are doing? Don't you have any manner to speak?" Ankita ma'am interrupted the police man.

"Who are you?" The police man asked.

"I am a medical professor," she said.

"Who is this young man with you?" he asked.

"He is my student," she replied.

"So you are planning to sleep with your student tonight?" one of them said sarcastically.

Robin at once got out of control and caught the collar of that policeman.

At once many police men rushed towards Robin and one of them slapped him saying, "Mother fucker you raised your hand on a policeman!"

"Stop this else I will lodge a complain against you people in DCP's office," ma'am shouted.

"Oh really! but before that I will carry all of you to the police station, still all night is left, we can have lots of fun, madam," a police man said ogling at ma'am.

Robin again tried to escape from their grip and thrash that policeman. Things were about to go out of control when suddenly an elderly police man came and asked us politely to pay the fine and leave. He demanded two thousand bucks. Ma'am threw the money on the face of one of them and they left threatening Robin not to mess with police. Ma'am offered five thousand rupees to Darpi which he accepted after a lot of persuasion. It was now 11:30 pm. Ma'am and Robin got into her car.

"Would you like to come to my place?" Ma'am asked.

Robin had all the desire of that but he didn't say anything. Ma'am then drove the car towards Sufdarjung Enclave. Robin was wondering whether ma'am will drop him at hostel or take him to her home. Soon his doubt cleared when madam turned in different direction from the hostel. After few minutes she stopped the car in front of a house in the posh Safdarjung Enclave.

# That night love crossed every Limit

"My flat is on the third floor of this apartment," ma'am said pointing up.

Ma'am parked the car in the basement and both walked towards the lift. The apartment seemed very plush. The lift opened at the third floor and ma'am turned to right and after few steps of walking she stopped at a door with name plate on which her name and designation were written in bold letters. She brought out the key from her purse and opened the lock and both got in. It was a three bed room flat with a drawing room and well equipped kitchen and a luxurious bathroom. Decoration and interior of room was like Robin had seen in Hindi films.

"Be comfortable I am just coming," ma'am said and entered a room.

Robin set on a sofa and looked around. A big plasma TV, a luxurious sofa and a few knick knacks were there in the drawing room. After five minutes ma'am came out combing her hair wearing a nightie which was sleeveless and up to her knees. It was pink but transparent. Robin could see the bra clearly. She sat carefully on sofa without revealing her inner thighs.

"Would you like to have tea or coffee?" ma'am asked.

"I usually take black coffee at night when I plan to wake all night," ma'am added.

"Are you planning to wake up all night?" Robin asked.

"Ya I plan to but if you feel sleepy you may go to sleep, there is no such restriction on you," ma'am smiled and went to the kitchen.

Ma'am started boiling water to make coffee. Sugar and coffee were on shelf where her hands could not reach. Ma'am tried several times to take it. Meanwhile Robin walked inside and saw madam struggling hard to get them. Her gown went up as she had over stretched her body to reach them. Robin's eyes stretched wide open to see the demanding thighs of ma'am. Robin looked above the thigh and her black panty became almost visible. He moved briskly into the kitchen and brought them down. While doing his body brushed against hers. "I am sorry ma'am."

Ma'am didn't say anything and poured sugar and coffee in two cups. Robin moved out of the kitchen. Ma'am came with cup of coffee and offered one to Robin. Unwillingly several times his eyes went on madam's beautiful sexy curves and several times he cursed himself for that.

"Ma'am... Who was Vishal Agnihotri?" he asked.

Ma'am took a long breath, waited for a minute and said, "He was my class mate."

"Were you in love with him?" Robin asked.

"Ya I did not know when our friendship turned into love, we had really a very good time together," she said pressing her back against the sofa.

"Where he is now? What happened? Why you didn't marry him?" Robin asked.

"It is a past thing now, I don't want to discuss it," madam said with a deep expiration.

"Ma'am I don't know if I am right or wrong but I loved you since the first time I saw you," Robin said looking at ma'am.

"Falling in love with a teacher is now common but one should not forget it is impossible to get it in real life," ma'am said.

"I knew it from the very first day Robin but I thought you will realize the reality and will soon act accordingly," she added.

"Ma'am when I saw you first time, you were not my teacher," Robin said and moved towards the window.

"I didn't get you?" ma'am said in confusion.

"Ma'am I saw you first in Lajpat Nagar market last year, you were dressed in blue jeans and a green top but before I could approach you, you drove away," Robin explained.

"My friends said if my love is true and my feelings are strong for you, you will definitely come to me someday."

"The girl with whom I fell in love was like other beautiful girls but it's my misfortune that she came to me as my teacher," he added and turned to madam.

"So when you first saw me in class you hit the desk and said it just because of frustration, was this your frustration?" ma'am asked.

"Ma'am I love you and want to be with you for ever," Robin said with wet eyes.

"Robin let me try the saari which you have designed for me," ma'am said changing the topic and went inside.

Robin swallowed the rest of the coffee in one sip. Ma'am came back in ten minutes wearing the sari. She was looking no less than a nymph.

"How I am looking?" she said and twirling around.

"Hear my heart beat and then you will know how you are looking?" Robin said and pulled ma'am towards him.

They became so close that their lips could touch each other any time. He curled his hands around ma'ams neck and pressed her head against his heart.

"Are you alright Robin?" ma'am said removing her ears from his chest.

"Do you need medicine? Your heart beat is not normal," she said.

Robin curled his right hand around ma'am's waist and pulled her closer and tried to kiss her. Ma'am resisted and Robin slackened his grip. Ma'am turned in the opposite direction and said, "There is something which is not known to you Robin."

"What ?" Robin asked.

"I am not Miss Ankita Srivastva, I am Mrs. Ankita Srivastva," she said hesitatingly.

"What... What did you say?" Robin stammered. "You are married?"

"Yes Robin, I am married to an industrialist Abhinav Jaiswal," she said.

Hearing this Robin let out a scream as if some one close had died, perhaps people react like this when the biggest dream of their life dies. It was no less than the funeral of his hope, love and life.

"Today you were shouting at some one on the phone, was it him? Robin asked crying.

"Yes Robin, he was my husband. He is calling me to Ahmadabad, where his family stays. He wants me to live there," she said sitting down on the sofa.

"Why were you shouting at him? He wants to live with you what's wrong with that?" Robin asked.

"I don't love him. In fact I hate him," she said pressing her fingers.

"What? Why did you get married with him then?" Robin asked in great surprise.

"It's not me but he who got married with me without my consent," Ma'am said.

"Wait, wait I don't get you," Robin said crying and pressing his head.

"I was in love with Vishal as you know. Abhinav is the son of my dad's best friend. His parents wanted me as their daughter in law. They asked for my hand from my father and one day Abhinav came to meet me and proposed for marriage. I told him every thing about me and Vishal and begged him to refuse me but he didn't do that. I couldn't resist my father and was forced to marry him."

"Did you have sex with your husband?" Robin asked.

"We had sex a couple of times when I met him, it was not a sex but an unwilling act to consummate our marriage, I am a female all restrictions are for me only" she said and burst into tears.

"I hate this society who doesn't listen to a girl and I hate my husband the most, he is the murderer of my love, now I will do what I like," she said defiantly.

"Ma'am... Please don't cry," Robin came near to ma'am and wiped her tears. It was raining outside but inside too there was nothing dry.

Ma'am looked at Robin and Robin at ma'am. Ma'am wiped his tears and he wiped madam's. The distance between their face started decreasing and then ma'am kept her lips on Robin's. They kissed each other passionately.

"I love you Robin," she uttered in between kissing.

"I love you too ma'am," Robin uttered.

They started taking off each others' clothes. Robin removed her sari which he had designed for ma'am. His hands stopped when they reached her bra.

"Robin don't stop, remove every thing and pour your love on to me," she said moaning with closed eyes.

"Ma'am I am not carrying any condoms," Robin said.

"Why do you need condoms?" ma'am asked.

"What if you get pregnant?" Robin said touching her genitals.

"Don't worry I will not get pregnant, I use contraceptive pills after sex with my husband," she said.

Robin at once removed all her clothes and lifted her in his arms. Ma'am showed him the way to her bed room. They became all naked and then they made love for another half an hour, becoming one body and soul and then fell on bed being all empty and exhausted. Robin was all content and looking up at the ceiling fan.

"Ma'am... why you didn't plan baby till today?" Robin asked kissing her breasts.

"I think baby should come when conjugal are in love, I mean they do sex to love not for fun," she answered with half closed eyes.

"Will you never plan a baby then?" Robin asked.

"Why don't you divorce your husband then?" Robin asked.

"Robin its not the time for such stupid discussions," she said and kissed his pubic areas desperately.

Again in a few minutes they were inside each other. That night was the most wonderful night in Robin's life.

# Trial love: I was in a girl's hostel

It was once again the season of Inter House competitions. Kabir House was the defending champion so at any cost it wanted to maintain its dominance. One night I got a call on my number from Charu.

"What are you doing?" she asked.

"My house wants me to play badminton for the Championship," I informed her.

"So are you planning to play for your house?" she asked.

"Yes definitely, last year too I represented my house, so it will be a matter of pride for me once again."

"I don't like you playing badminton in shorts," she said.

"Don't play badminton for your house," she said.

I was totally astonished hearing her.

"My house needs me and above all I love playing badminton," I said.

"It means you don't love me. Isn't it?" she said.

181

"It is not that," I tried to explain.

"Either me or your stupid badminton... decision is all yours," she said and hung up.

"Oh fuck... what she is doing with me now-a-days? My life has become out of control," I shouted and hit the door.

Her last line was striking my head like a hammer. Lastly I took a decision which was expected from a lover. I withdrew myself from the championship. My house members were all wonderstruck by this decision of mine. Some of them even criticized me for that and I could see a wave of hatred on every body's face for me. Robin was also not happy but he didn't say anything. Need not to say this time the badminton trophy went to Nanak house. Nanak house organized a small party at night for winning the trophy. I was restless as every body in my house was very sad and I was cursing myself for falling in love. Around 11 o' clock night I got a phone call from Charu.

"What are you doing honey" she asked.

"Nothing... just trying to sleep,"

"Why so early? Are you alright?" she asked.

"I am alright but a little restless."

"I know it is all because of me. Kabir house lost because you didn't play. I know how much you are associated with this game and how much you are suffering right now," she expressed her care.

"Come to me, don't be alone. You need me; I am all alone in my room." she invited.

"What? How can I come to you at this time and that too in your room?" I asked in wonder.

"Not a big deal. No one is in the hostel and you can come by climbing the pole at the back side of the hostel" she explained.

"Charu... I don't have any experience of climbing poles, so leave it. Moreover it is dangerous and risky," I said.

"Every thing is done the first time. No one is born with experience. Can't you do it for me, many guys come to meet their girl friends," she said complaining.

"Charu it is risky, if security will see, admin will throw me out of this medical college," I tried to reason with her.

"Nothing will happen, I assure you so come fast. I am dying to see you," she said and disconnected.

I never knew why she used to disconnect the phone after making me hear her verdict, perhaps she was sure I will do whatever she will ask and she was not wrong. When I was talking to Charu, Robin heard parts of it.

"Where are you going?" He asked.

"Charu has called me in her room right now?" I said.

"You will go into a girl's hostel? Do you know the consequences if you are caught?" he shouted.

"Yes, I know but I am doing all this because of love," I tried to make him understand.

"She is using you damn it. She doesn't love you. Is this called love?" he said.

"I don't know what she is doing is love or not but I am doing what is called love," I explained.

"Stop this nonsense Raj, love is not hurting someone and playing with sentiments," he said.

"She may be playing on the name of love but it was me who agreed for trial love now I can't withdraw myself," I explained.

"You are not a Rajput damn it" he shouted.

"It is not an ego, it is just a promise made by love for love, so don't stop me," I said and left.

For the past three months I was doing what I used to be asked to do by Charu. My life was not mine any more, it was totally out of control. I was standing near the pole. I looked up in order to evaluate the height of the third floor where Charu was staying. Before climbing the pole I gave a missed call to Charu. She came to guide and guard my way. I slipped many times but somehow managed to reach the third floor. She then led me to her room. It was really a nice well decorated room with a girly atmosphere and items. Her roommate was not in the room. Charu was dressed in a sky colored synthetic nightie.

"You have proved you love me very much," she said caressing my head.

She put on a very romantic song from "Raaju Ban Gaya Gentleman" and came and sat close to me.

"So if you understood the fact that I love you very much what's your decision regarding my proposal?" I asked.

"Don't ask me for my decision, ask me for my desire?" she asked.

I looked at her with confusion. Needless to say she was looking very hot and now her voice turned husky and very sexy, something which I did not expect.

"I want to give you something which is worth more than my confirmation," she said.

She clutched my head from the back and pulled me towards her. Our lips were about to close on each other when she pushed me on the bed. She jumped at me and started kissing my neck. Oh my God I can't explain how wonderful it felt. All I can say it was like a four hundred twenty volt current running through my body. She unbuttoned my shirt and threw it away.

"Charu... do you know what you are doing?" I asked closing my eyes.

"I know everything, you can do anything for me and can't I do some thing for you?" she said and kept kissing my neck.

"Are you sure you want to do it?" I again asked.

She didn't say anything and unhooked my trousers and threw it away too. I had only underwear on in the name of a cloth on me. She kept her one hand between her boobs and one on my pelvis. I curled my hands around her back and tried to kiss her. Suddenly someone knocked at the door. We were in panic.

"Who is there?" I whispered.

"How I am supposed to know? Hide under the bed," she said and moved towards the door.

I went under the bed. Suddenly I saw my clothes lying on the floor and as I was to come out to collect it, Charu opened the door. A girl came in and asked Charu something. Thanks God she didn't see my clothes and she went away. Charu locked the door again and again a new spell of love making started. I started leaking and anytime I was to thrust myself into Charu when there was a knock again on the door. It seemed few girls were at the door.

"Put on your clothes," she commanded.

I started putting them on and cursing those girls. She tied her hair quickly and moved towards the door. I went under bed once again.

"Why you took so much time to open the door?" one girl asked.

"I was sleeping" she said.

"With whom?" one giggled and asked.

"Perhaps with the lucky guy who is under the bed," another girl said and my heart stopped to beat.

"Raj... Come out. We have been caught," Charu said and all started laughing.

I came out sheepishly and then I realized every thing. It was all Charu's plan.

"So you got anything or not?"Someone among them asked me laughing.

It was no less than a humiliation.

"O shut up... He is a nice guy," Charu pretended to scold her and laughed.

"Go back to your hostel Raj, I will see you tomorrow," Charu ordered me out as though I was her pet dog and I obeyed like I was her dog.

No matter how much committed you are to your love sometimes when you get hurt you curse yourself for falling in love. At this time a doubt started emerging in my mind whether I had chosen the right girl. Charu had humiliated me many times before many people earlier, but this was the first time when I felt bad about loving her. I returned to my hostel. Robin was not in the room. He had left a slip for me on which was written, "I will stay tonight with Ankita ma'am." I tore it to shreds and became jealous of Robin's luck. I was jealous all night that he was making love to Ankita ma'am and here I had humiliated to this level when I was just naked. Robin had started sleeping with ma'am almost every night. He always made love without condoms.

# Trial Love: I became a puppet

It was the final cricket match between Kabir and Nanak house. Our house won the toss and elected to bat first. Robin and I were to leave for opening our innings any time. Suddenly I got a call from Charu.

"Honey I need you very much, come to me," she said.

"Charu I have a match right now and I am going to bat," I informed her.

"I don't feel well and you are interested in cricket? Shame on you," she shouted.

"What happened to you?" I asked.

"Vomiting and stomach pain, I need to visit a doctor"

"And don't ask me to manage myself, but if your cricket is more important to you then leave me to die," she added and disconnected.

"Charu…Charu," I shouted

Robin looked at me suspiciously. I took out my helmet and gloves and looked at Robin.

"No..You can't do this" he shouted.

"I will have to, it's an emergency, and she needs me," I said and ran with my maximum speed out of the room. Soon there was a panic in Kabir house management. I reached Indira hostel and called Charu. She came and it seemed she really was in trouble.

"Where you would like to go for a check up?" I asked.

"Let's go to Rockland hospital in Qutub Industrial area," she suggested.

I drove the bike through Ber Sarai and reached Rockland Hospital. I parked my bike.

"Lets sit for a while here," Charu said pointing to its cafeteria.

I was confused with her suggestion. I left my house in a pathetic condition just for her and here she was saying that we sit in a cafeteria. I didn't react and I followed her to the cafeteria. At its entry she stood for a while touched her tummy, pressed it and declared, "Now I am feeling alright."

"Raj its your company, I am alright now. I want to eat something," she said.

"The Cafeteria is all yours, order what you want," I said.

"Not here, let's go to Barista at Priya," she suggested.

"Charu if you are alright can we go back to the campus as there's still sometime when I can contribute for my house," I begged.

"I knew it... Nothing is more important than cricket in your life," she said sounding disappointed.

"Its not like that..." I said and touched Charu's shoulders but she shook herself away.

"Don't touch me, now you realise why I took such a long time to think upon your proposal," she said.

"I am sorry, I had no intention to hurt you. Let's go to Priya," I said and moved towards the parking lot.

I drove thinking all the way about my screwed up life. At one end Charu was standing and at another end all my freedom and dreams. At this particular point of time I had nothing with me. I was a loser. We went to Barista and had a cup of coffee. By the time we returned to our campus Kabir house had lost one more championship because of me. I returned to my room hiding my face. Due to guilt I was dying every minute. Charu meantime again won the painting competition and this time she was once again the candidate for Miss Medico, representing Nanak house. I never revealed my disappointment to Charu and supported her in every possible way but she kept humiliating me. Now she attacked my liking towards chicken . I promised her to become a pure vegetarian. Meanwhile she cleared all the rounds of Miss Medico competition and won the title. She was looking the most beautiful girl in the world wearing the crown made up of American diamonds and waving her hands in order to thank the crowd . She looked very happy and when I saw her happiness all my disappointment melted away. I felt very happy. She looked many times at me from the stage. It was a great time for Nanak house. Nanak house threw a big party in which every body was invited. I with Robin went there too. I bought a red rose for my lady. I came to her and handed over the rose to her but she just kept it on the table taking little interest in the flower or me. Soon the DJ started the party rocking and every body went to the dance floor. Charu was dancing with her class mates. I couldn't bear the pain and gulped down several pegs of vodka. Robin called up Ankita ma'am several times but she didn't pick up his phone. He looked upset and drank a lot. We left the party soon as there was nothing there to hold us back. Charu started making me realize that she was now Miss Medico and it was a matter of pride for her not to date the most ordinary guy and above all a junior. I tried a lot but could not manage to bridge the gap which had arisen. We used to meet rarely now and phone calls were also not that frequent as earlier. Robin was restless to see Ankita ma'am who was neither coming to college nor picking up his phone. Rahul's life was a bit normal but Shivani's Asst manager was still a problem who used to ogle at Shivani now more intensively without any fear as he was not asst manager now but got promoted and become Manager. Charu was already in her final year and not much time was left for her to pass out. Ankita ma'am was replaced by a new obstetrics teacher. There were rumors that she was pregnant and was on maternity leave.

# Trial Love: I am nowhere... broken

One night Charu called me up on my number and asked me to meet her. She seemed grief stricken. She asked me to come right away to the back of canteen, the place where I had proposed to her. Considering the place, I was filled with a sense of anticipation that perhaps something was going to happen in my favor. Robin too called up Ankita ma'am and this time after several rings she picked his phone.

"Ma'am where are you and why you are not picking my phone?" he asked desperately.

I could hear only what Robin was saying. Robin begged her many times to meet just once, and finally she relented.

It was the month of February; there was a nip in the air. I reached Subhash's canteen at 8 o' clock in the evening. I saw Charu sitting near the statue. As she saw me, she ran towards me and hugged me tightly. I didn't know how to react.

"I was dying to see you, to touch you," she said.

"Raj...I wronged you greatly. I am sorry for everything," she said and again hugged me.

"I have made you suffer all the time since you proposed to me," she added tearfully.

"What is love? What you did for me is the standard definition of love without any interest," she added.

"Charu it's Ok. I have all the interests in you, I just want to convince you I am your real soul mate," I said wiping her tears.

"This trial love was my fault, I lost you for ever," she said.

"After Miss Medico's competition I wanted to express my feeling for you. Even I loved you always but I just wanted to check how much you respect and love me."

"Then why you didn't express it to me, why you tormented me all these days?" I asked.

"Because my uncle has chosen a guy for me and he wants me to marry him," she said.

"What? And what have you thought?" I asked fearfully.

"I tried to convince my uncle for you but he didn't agree," she said.

"If you love me, why you are caring for your uncle?" I asked and became tearful.

"Because my uncle has supported us in every possible way after the death of my father, what I am today is just because of him," she explained.

"We are very much obligated to him and he wants me to marry a Kolkata based Bengali surgeon," she explained.

"It means you are all set to fire me for your uncle's debt?" I shouted.

"I suffered all the time in the hope that some day you will love me and today you are saying me all these crap," I shouted and hit my hand against a mirror placed there.

My hand got badly injured and started bleeding.

"Please don't hurt yourself, I have already hurt you a lot," she said and tied her hanky on my wrist.

I gripped her cheeks from both sides and said, "Please don't leave me, I promise I will do everything for your happiness."

We both were helpless, she due to her values and me due to my great love for her. We didn't know when our lips met and we kissed each other so deeply that our tongues stroked each other. Suddenly her grip slackened and my eyes opened. She pushed me away.

"We are doing what is not possible Raj, stay away from me," she cried and ran away.

I could not do anything except seeing her disappear not only from my sight but from my life gradually and then completely. My body lost all its strength and I fell near the statue, crying and looking at the sky and cursing my luck and God. The world seemed all colorless for me.

# Cruel Intention behind a beautiful face

It was not just me who was suffering; someone else was to suffer too now. Robin and Ma'am met near the old library which used to be secluded all the time. Ankita ma'am opened the door of her car and took much time to get out of it. When Robin saw her he was totally astonished. Ankita ma'am was still very beautiful but the change was only her huge belly.

"Ma'am, you are pregnant?" Robin asked in astonishment.

"Yes Robin I am 6 months pregnant," ma'am informed.

"It means the rumors about your pregnancy were right," Robin said."But you said you had no plans to have a baby?" Robin said.

"I had said baby should come when two persons are in love and they do sex for making love not fun," she said.

"So you forgave your husband and now you are in love with him," Robin asked in agony.

"I still hate my husband but this baby is the fruit of my love with a lovely person," she said.

"What? It means this baby is mine?" Robin exclaimed.

"Yes Robin this baby is yours," ma'am informed him.

"But you had told me that you are taking contraceptive pills to avoid pregnancy?" Robin reminded her.

"Yes I had told you but did you ever see me taking those pills?" Ma'am asked.

"It means you cheated me?" Robin shouted.

"No one cheats no one Robin, this is life — we sometimes become a medium," she said.

"Now I will tell you the ultimate truth," she said.

"What is it?" Robin asked.

"I was in love with a guy whom I couldn't marry. It was just because of my husband. He assured me to reject me but he didn't. He spoilt my life. After marriage every girl wants to be a mother but I didn't because I never loved my husband. I saw you interested in me and somehow I got attracted to you and your love for me. I loved you and then I planned to fulfill my will to be a mother," Ma'am explained.

"It's alright ma'am, but if you love me then leave and divorce your husband. I want to marry you, I can do anything for you," Robin declared.

"Giving my husband divorce and marrying will not serve my purpose and it will be like I forgave my husband for his betrayal," ma'am said with a mysterious smile.

"You are much younger to me so there is no question of marriage, but if a guy is mature enough to produce semen, he can make pregnant a much older female," she said in one breath.

"You served a few of my purposes. First I was dying to get loved by an innocent lover, secondly who can make me pregnant by convincing me to fall in love with him, third who can give me a goal to lead the rest of my life with my husband," she explained.

"You don't love your husband and yet you want to spend the rest of your life with him?" Robin asked in wonderment.

"I want to live with him to see him suffering and so I can enjoy this baby which is not his but he will consider it as his own and when he will become as old not to get someone pregnant I will tell him the truth," she disclosed.

"This is not a baby, it is his suffering which is getting nourished in my uterus, and for me this is my golden moments with you," she said.

"You have lost what you had, why are you spoiling your life just in nurturing hatred, I promise you I will fulfill all of your expectations" Robin said and caressed her hair.

"I love you Robin but my hatred for my husband is far deeper and stronger than my love for you. This baby doesn't belong to Jaiswal's khandaan but certainly it is a full stop to Abhinav Jaiswal's khandan," she said and laughed like a vamp.

"It means you didn't love me and just used me for your revenge, I became your scapegoat," Robin shouted.

"Robin you got what you wanted, you wanted to love me and I offered you my body and in turn I received your semen and got pregnant and in this way my revenge got completed, what's wrong in it?" she cleared.

"I didn't love you for your body, but you played with my emotions, my love, my sentiments," Robin shouted.

"It happens in life with every one sooner or later, it is our last meeting, we will not meet now, I am going back Ahmadabad to stay with my husband and his family with your life time gift to me," she said and kissed Robin.

They kissed each other for a life time as this was going to be their last kiss. After five minutes ma'am turned towards her car.

"Ma'am don't leave me alone, I can't live without you" Robin said and ran after her car but by then she had driven away. "Ma'am I will die without you and my child," he shouted running behind her car and then fell down..

The calm young night suddenly shook with the screams of the two friends who had lost their loves just now.

We came back to our hostel. We saw each other and rushed to each other, hugged and cried a lot. We understood everything which just passed through us. It was the closure of the chapter called love which had knocked and entered in our world, rocked our lives and eloped leaving us all with shattered dreams and a hopeless life.

# Destiny of Two soul mates: Part II

Like everyday Shivani went to her office. She came to her desk and started arranging her things.

"Good morning Shivani," she was greeted by Rashmi.

"Hey...Good morning. How are you?" Shivani asked.

"Fine... What about you? Everything set for marriage?" Rashmi asked.

"Ya... It's a dream which is just to come true," she chuckled.

"Dreams never come true Shivani," Rashmi said and opened the file of the customers.

"Shivani a few staff got promotion and I too figure among them," she informed.

"Promotion? But why they didn't promote me, I am senior to you?" Shivani asked in astonishment.

"I don't have any idea, perhaps Kanut is not happy with you," Rashmi said.

"Is he happy with you?" Shivani asked with a tough look.

"Hey by the way I am throwing a party at my house this evening and you have to come at any cost," she declared.

"I can't come, I have to meet my would be in-laws today," she lied.

"If you will not come I am going to cancel the party," Rashmi said sounding disappointed.

A little argument followed and finally Shivani agreed to come. Shivani called Rahul on phone and informed him about everything. After office Shivani went to Rashmi's house. The house was all dead with no body.

"Where have your parents gone?" Shivani asked.

"They have gone to Shirdi for darshan that's why I have thrown the party at home, you know how costly other places are?" She said.

Shivani nodded her head.

"Let's have a drink yaar?" Rashmi said.

She opened the door of refrigerator and took out a Kingfisher beer bottle. Shivani was surprised seeing her having beer.

"What the hell is this?" Shivani asked.

"This is life darling," Rashmi said poured beer in a glass.

"Since when have you started drinking?" Shivani asked.

"Since I started thinking about my carrier, my life" she said and looked at Shivani.

"I will not take wine and don't force me as I am still very strong regarding my principles and you will get hurt" Shivani said with confidence.

Shivani switched on the TV and started surfing channels. It was 10 o' clock. Shivani looked at her watch and said "If there is a party here why have people not turned up?"

"Soon every body will turn up, don't take tension," she said pouring some more beer in her glass.

"So you will not take beer, no problem I will bring you some cold drink," she said and turned towards the refrigerator.

She fetched Pepsi in a glass after five minutes. Shivani started taking sip. It was now 11 o' clock and no body had turned up.

"My head is aching like hell," Shivani informed Rashmi.

"If you are not Ok take rest in my room," she suggested.

Suddenly the door bell rang. Rashmi moved briskly to the door. She opened the door and Kanut entered. Shivani opened her eyes and she saw them whispering very seriously.

She looked at her watch and it was 11:30, she realized every thing. Tears started streaming out of her eyes. Kanut came to her and sat by her side.

"Shivani please don't mind, I guess everything is known to you now, but what else could I do to get you?" he said. Shivani was glaring at Rashmi continuously. Rashmi looked down.

"I approached you several times but you didn't care a little then I approached this bitch who is your best friend" he said and touched Shivani's lips.

"This asshole has already slept with me for the promotion and even ambushed your friendship," he again touched her lips and wanted to touch her breasts.

Shivani slapped him tightly and stood up; drops of tears fell on the floor.

"She is a weak lady but how dare you generalize it Kanut, my every breath belongs to Rahul." she shouted holding up her head.

"Shivani I will not mind attempting rape on you today," Kanut said and came closer. As he stepped forward a few steps towards Shivani, she ran towards the balcony of the  house and suddenly jumped from the seven storey building. Both Rashmi and Kanut looked down from there and they could see nothing except a body lying still on the road. Soon Shivani was carried to AIIMS but due to the scarcity of bed which is a life time fucking problem of hospital like AIIMS, she was transported to DIMS, in other words our college's hospital. She was soon admitted to ICU on life support system. Five of her bones got multiple fractures with a moderate head injury. Doctors started struggling to save her life and we started praying for our sister. Rahul became half mad. He used to burst in tears while thinking of Shivani. If you don't have money, you can have nothing. This is the basic thing which I knew and observed it implies every where. Highly commercial hospitals have no care for your lives but they care only for money. Doctor declared Shivani needed a surgery urgently as one of her ribs just penetrated her liver a little. The total cost which the hospital put forward was ten lacs. It was an impossible amount for a poor family like Rahul's and Shivani's. They lost all hopes and started counting days when they will be informed about Shiavni's departure to another world.

Robin asked his father to help them but these politicians I tell you are worth nothing. He abruptly refused and even asked Robin to keep out of it. I wondered how come Robin was born to such a selfish man. It was the day when Robin for the first time confronted his father and broke his bond with his father. His father hardly cared about it.  It happens only in Indian politics where emotions and relationships have no place. We were all shattered and broken and not a single ray of hope was visible. Suddenly Rahul's mobile rang.

"Hello... Who is it?" Rahul asked.

Then I don't know, Rahul didn't speak anything and listened for another five minutes and then he moved out of Shivani's ward keeping the mobile close to his ears. I came out of the ward to go to the toilet and as I turned towards the toilet I saw Rahul exchanging serious words with a fifty year old woman. She was wearing a black burkha.

I entered in and passed water for another two complete minutes and was biting my brain in order to identify that woman. Suddenly one of my nerve got stimulated and it gave me the information which I was seeking. She was Firoza Jalaal, an employee in the hospital who was the in charge of sanitation of hospital and had joined the hospital just three month ago.

Rahul came back in the ward and looked at Shivani for long and tears which had become our lives started making misfortune's presence felt. Robin and I consoled him and then we went to the canteen to have our lunch. Food was no longer fun but for the sake of health and formality we had to take it. Rahul swallowed not more than two gulps and suddenly moved towards wash basin and washed his hands.

"I am going home, I guess I need to rest," he said.

We did not say anything and he left. I and Robin spent three hours in canteen with a grief afflicted face and brain working constantly as to how to manage the huge money for our sister. We had never been silent so long in our history.

We came back to the hospital's waiting room; suddenly TV started displaying breaking news "Three bomb blast in a series took at least thirty lives and hundreds of injury in a packed market of Sarojini Nagar". We didn't know how to react to this news as we had not seen anything except suffering since ages. Suddenly I saw Shivani's mother standing at the reception signing a few papers. She saw me and asked me to come with her. I went there and to my utmost surprise she was signing on surgery document.

"Have you paid the money aunty?" I asked.

"No son, I have been called by the lady at the reception to sign the paper regarding the surgery," she informed.

"Who paid that high amount then?" I mumbled.

I asked the receptionist but she refused to divulge any information about the donor. She just said it came from some institution, perhaps from a Muslim organization. We further interrogated but she didn't tell us anything due to the fucking confidential policy. Any way we were happy that a big problem had sorted out by itself. I could see a level of satisfaction on Shivani's mother's face as in between my interrogation she several times mumbled "God is there so are good human beings too,"

*I had never been in such an emergency. It is probably the worst day of my life so far. Shivani was already in ICU with coma and now Rahul too had got hospitalized. He was badly injured in Sarojni nagar bomb blast which just took many lives with hundreds of injuries. ......*

Rahul's condition was severe but he started responding to treatment and so did Shivani. It seemed that they wanted to live and fulfill their dream. Love got victory over every thing, even death. Only love can create such magic. After a month they were as stable and able to talk to us. When Rahul was bed ridden I saw only tears in his eyes when ever he looked at us. He used to ask about Shivani with his expressionless face by just his eyes.

# Terror its network & India

One month later, when Rahul could talk to us, he said, "I have a long story to tell"

"We want to know everything," I said.

"Why you went Sarojini Nagar, the day the bomb blast took place?" Robin asked.

"I was the one behind this bomb blast" he said and burst into tears.

"What...." I and Robin said in unison.

We were just motionless and helpless or you may say we didn't want to believe the fact.

Rahul looked at us and screamed, "I have taken hundreds of live for the sake of my love"

Robin realized the situation and hugged Rahul and so did I.

"How you got entrapped in it?" I asked.

"That is what I want to tell you people as I am dying every day with my guilt," Rahul said wiping his tears.

"Do you guys remember the day when we were all very tensed about Shivani's medical fee and then suddenly I got a call and I went out of the ward leaving you?" he asked.

"Yes we remember," we said in unison.

"I had got a call from a person who denied telling his name, he was aware of our problem. He offered to pay Shivani's fee if I could do one task for him," he said.

"What was the task?" Robin asked.

"He asked me to contact Firoza Jalaal, he gave me a pass word for contact it was something "kiss me or kill me"

"What? Kiss me or kill me? Was it a password?"

"I left you people in ward and went to contact Firoza as he had given me a clear instruction that I should do everything by myself without any body's help," he added.

"Firoza described me my task, it was very easy, I had to transfer a bag from Khanpur to Sarojini Nagar, and she gave me the address from where I had to pick up the bag."

"I picked the bag which was not very big but was quite heavy as compared to its size. He asked me to transfer the bag to a person in Sarojini Nagar near Roli's restaurant," he said.

"How did you recognize that person?" I asked.

"I was told that a man will come to me and pronounce the same password and in turn I was to pronounce to match up" Rahul informed.

I was totally wonderstruck by the network which terrorists had created to destroy our country.

"I kept waiting there but no one came to me at the given time which was 5 in the evening."

"I opened the bag which was not allowed and I was totally shocked to see a time bomb inside," he said breaking into tears.

"Oh my God…" I and Robin said in unison.

"I tried to get the bomb out of the market but I could not as a very few minutes were left in the regulating meter so I dropped the bag in the park where a few people were walking and ran away silently but the bomb got blasted before I could leave the place completely and I got injured on the way" he said fighting back his tears.

"This was the story of my crime and guilt and I hate myself for taking the lives of innocent lives," he hit his fist on the wall.

Robin went near to Rahul and said, "I don't think you have committed any crime."

Both Rahul and me looked at him inquiringly.

"Yes Rahul… the bomb had to blast anyway and if you were not the medium these guys would have found some one else for this purpose as India is a country of unemployment and needs," Robin justified.

I agreed with his justification.

"A few arrests have been made by the police and now the case is totally in the cold box so you don't worry for anything" I said consoling Rahul.

"I am not worried about punishment I am worried about my sin."

"You have not done anything sinful actually you have done a pious act," Robin said.

"You saved a life out of this blast."

"Hundreds of lives had to be in the gulp of Yamraaj anyway but you have dragged out one life from his mouth, isn't it a pious act?" Robin asked.

Anyhow we managed to console Rahul and dragging him out of this trauma as he was still recovering.

Shivani was discharged from hospital. Their marriage got postponed for few months as Shivani was still very weak.

# At last: Unusual End

Time passed and the day of convocation came of Chart. It was a packed hall in which Charu was to be awarded for her excellent performance all the years. Her mother, uncle, brother including her would- be had come to participate and they all looked very proud.

Ankita ma'am was also to get the farewell as she was leaving for Ahmedabad the day after, her husband was also present. Robin and I were standing at the end of the hall looking at our past. The convocation started and we came out. Suddenly we heard a baby scream. Robin looked back. Ankita ma'am came out trying to soothe her baby. She saw Robin and stood motionless. They looked at each other for a long time and I moved away from there.

"Robin… have a look at our baby," she said looking down at the baby.

"Is it a girl or a boy?" Robin asked.

"A beautiful girl," ma'am answered.

"She looks like you," she informed.

"I hope she will have all my qualities rather than yours," Robin said with a sigh.

"I have a question… how you convinced your husband that it was his hard work?"

"My husband is a good human being. Perhaps he has committed a single mistake which I guess is a crime so he will be punished all his life and the main thing is that he is an emotional fool," ma'am said.

"The day I conceived, I decided to call my husband to Delhi. He ran and came cancelling all his appointments and deals and like usual I had sex with him for the next two days."

"He went back to Ahmadabad and after ten days I informed him that I was pregnant."

"He was happy and ask me to come to Ahmadabad which was expected and I agreed as this was what I had planned" she said.

"Guys are really fools in a few cases I guess," she chuckled.

"Yes… Because there are a few people who think women are not all fun but the blessing of God, anyway, can I hold my daughter?" Robin asked and looked at the baby.

As Robin held his baby he burst into tears. Ma'am turned away hurriedly.

"Don't acquire your mother's qualities beta," he said crying.

Soon people started coming out of the hall as the convocation was over. Abhinav Jaiswal joined Ma'am and she took away the baby from Robin's lap and walked away with her husband. Robin was like he would die any moment. I ran to him and hugged him tightly. Soon Charu came out with her family and would- be, who was a well built man but seemed somewhat old. He had a well marked mustache and oily hair and like most Bengalis he was having problem in speaking Hindi. Suddenly my eyes went teary and I looked at Charu whom I had lost to this oily haired old Bengali. Charu looked at me and she too went teary and soon left with her family. I did not dare to even congratulate her lest I did something foolish

In the month of June, Rahul and Shivani got married. At least something good happened to them and we were all delighted to see the happy ending of our friend and sister. They looked fortunate and blessed.

# From Bottom of my heart:

Teri hasrato se sazi

Meri apni duniya me main rahoo,

Teri berukhi se darta hai dil

Chaahat apni kaise tumhe main kahoo.

Ye hawa tumhe chhoo kar

Mujhe har pal jalati hai,

Ye bunde bearish ki tumhe bhigo ke

Mujhe har pal satati hai.

Inko bina mange ye haq mila

Maine to har pal band hothon se Guzaarish ki,

Apne dil ki hi sun lo

Tere dil ne bhi mere pyaar ki sifarish ki.

Maana tum khuda ki anuthi kriti ho

Dharti bhi tere kadmo ko chumti hai,

Chaand ka noor bhi fika hai tere saamne

Husn ki paribhasha bhi tere ird gird hi Ghoomti hai.

E Khuda apni amaanat mujhe de de

Teri banayi ye duniya ab mehfooz nahi,

Haath faila nahi sakta ab aur kahin

Ho jane de dil ki milawate ab yahi.